KEEPING
Katie

SYNDICATE KINGS

KATE OLIVER

This book is a work of fiction. Names, characters, organizations, places, events, and incidents are either a product of the author's imagination or are used fictitiously. Any resemblance to actual persons, living or dead, businesses, companies, events, or locales is entirely coincidental.

Written by: Kate Oliver
Cover Designer: Scott Carpenter

Copyright © 2024 Kate Oliver

"ALL RIGHTS RESERVED. This book contains material protected under International and Federal Copyright Laws and Treaties. Any unauthorized reprint or use of this material is prohibited. No part of this book may be reproduced or transmitted in any form or by any means, electronic or mechanical, including photocopying, recording, or by any information storage and retrieval system without express written permission from the author/publisher."

CONTENT WARNINGS

This book is a DD/lg romance. The MMC in this book is a Daddy Dom and the MFC identifies as a Little. This is an act of role-playing and/or a lifestyle dynamic between the characters and falls under the BDSM umbrella. This is a consensual power exchange relationship between adults. In this story there are spankings and discussions of other forms of discipline.

Additional content warning

Assault
Death of parents and siblings

Please do not read this story if you find any of this to be disturbing or a trigger for you.

1
GRADY

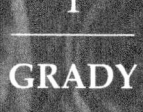

"What are you watching?"

It was only a matter of time before she showed up.

Turning to the large archway that leads into the room, I raise an eyebrow. "What are you doing up, Little girl? You're supposed to be in bed."

Cali's lips curve into a mischievous smile. "Grady, we both know when Daddy's away, I'm going to come down and make you switch from the boring news to *Friends*. It's a tradition. I don't know why you're surprised. It's just silly."

My chest warms, and it's not from the whiskey. This sassy Little girl is a handful, but God, I love her. She came into this family like a little ray of sassy sunshine and made all of us fall in love with her. The sister some of us never had.

"Cali Ann, you really need your butt spanked more." I wink and point to the other end of the couch. "Come lie down."

She bounces on her toes as she makes her way into the room, her messy hair swaying with her movements, then lowers herself and her stuffed wolf to the cushions. I grab one of the blankets we always have draped over the back for nights like this and toss it over her. Then I find *Friends* on the TV and relax against the cushions with a sigh. She may be married to my boss, but this companionship between us fills my cup in a way I need more than I'd like to admit.

"Why couldn't you sleep?" I watch as she fidgets to get comfortable.

"I never sleep when Daddy's gone. I worry about him. Why are you up still?" She shifts her brown eyes toward me, searching my face.

That's the million-dollar question I wish I had the answer to. Sleep has been hard to come by lately. It's aggravating.

"Probably because I knew there would be a Little troublemaker coming down here at some point."

She nudges my thigh with her toe, her face red as she laughs. "You love it. Don't even try to deny it. Our quality time together is special."

Sneaking my hand under the blanket, I run the tips of my fingers along the sole of her foot. As soon as I do, she squeals and twists, kicking at my hand to get away from the tickles.

"Grady! That's not nice." She mock-glares at me, but the grin she's trying to conceal gives her away. "You're never gonna find a girl of your own if you're mean all the time. Tickling is basically torture, and nobody wants to be tortured."

Tilting my head to the side, I narrow my gaze. "Says the Little girl who talked about cutting off fingers and feeding people to the fishes when she moved in."

"Well, it was really disappointing to find out that a bunch of badass mafia guys don't resort to old-school techniques like they did in the good ol' days."

My chest shakes as I try to control my laughter. "Good ol' days? You were part of a lot of those, huh, lass?"

She lets out a deep, dramatic sigh and rolls her eyes. "You're changing the subject. We were talking about how you need to find a woman. Do you want my help? I can set up a dating profile or something. Maybe take some pictures of you looking," she motions to my suit, "less murder-y and more normal."

"Murder-y?" I'm barely keeping myself together. Cali has become so full of life since she married Declan. I love that she feels safe around all of us. Cali, Scarlet, Chloe, and Paisley—they all do. These women have somehow wormed their way into our cold, black hearts and turned all of Declan's men into putty for them.

"Okay, you know what? You're obviously not taking this conversation seriously, so I'll set up a profile for you tomorrow on mafiamatch.com."

The smile disappears from my face, quickly replaced with a scowl. "Cali Ann, if you even think of making me a profile on mafiamatch or any fucking dating site, app, or swiping program, I will spank your bare ass myself. Are we clear?"

Her mouth falls open, and she stares at me in silence for several seconds. Probably trying to figure out if I'm being serious or not. Most of the time, I'm pretty easygoing with the girls, but if she sets up a dating profile for me, I'll follow through on that threat. As long as my boss approves, of course. Which, considering he's a jealous bastard, he won't. But he'd probably do it for me, so that's good enough.

"Sheesh! Okay, Mr. Grumpypants, I won't make you a dating profile… yet. But I think you should consider it. You need to find someone before you get old and wrinkly and your balls fall off."

Lord, this one is trying my nerves tonight. "My balls won't ever fall off. And stop worrying about my dating life. Do I look like I need help finding someone?"

She gives me a once over, and I can't help the flicker of insecurity I feel. I'm not sure why. I could have my pick of women. The problem is, so far, I haven't been able to find a woman I've wanted to pick. I guess the second issue is that, I haven't even been looking.

"I suppose not, but I've never seen you date anyone."

Pinching the bridge of my nose, I let out a long, controlled breath. "Just because you've never seen it doesn't mean I haven't."

I might be blowing smoke, but it's better than admitting that the only thing tending to my needs lately has been my right hand.

"So you just don't bring them here? Are you ashamed of us? We wouldn't be mean to anyone."

My gut twists, and I sit up straighter. "Why the hell would I be ashamed of you girls? Who the fuck made you even think such a thing?"

Cali isn't used to me snapping at her. None of the women are, actually. That's usually left for Kieran or Ronan to do. Sometimes Killian.

"No one did. I just don't know why you haven't brought anyone to the estate to meet us. We'd welcome anyone you dated into our circle. We just want all of you guys to be happy. You're a good man, Grady. You deserve to be loved just as much as anyone else."

Jesus, fuck. Cali is pulling all the emotional strings today. Reaching out, I wrap my fingers around her ankle and squeeze. "When I meet the right one, I'll introduce her to you girls. I'm not ashamed of you. Although I am a little concerned your naughtiness might rub off on another woman."

The light in her eyes begins to flicker again. "It's not naughtiness, it's charisma. Duh, silly."

I wink at her and set my drink on the table next to the couch. "If you say so, Little one. Go to sleep. Your Daddy is going to be mad at me if you don't get enough rest."

She turns her attention to the TV and clutches the stuffed wolf to her chest. She'll be out in no time, and when Declan gets home, he'll carry her up to bed like he always does.

A few minutes pass, the laugh track of the show permanently ingrained in my mind. She nudges me with her toe again. I turn my head to look at her, she smiles softly.

"Love you, Grady. Thanks for putting up with me and my bullshit all the time."

It takes a second and several swallows before I give her a slight nod. "Love you too, Little one. And no cursing. Go ni-night."

With a sigh, she closes her eyes. It only takes minutes before her breathing evens out and her arms go slack. I'm left staring at her while replaying our conversation in my head.

At my age, I should have settled down with someone. Being in the mafia and living a long life aren't two things that typically go together. If mob statistics were a thing, I'd probably be considered past middle age even though I'm only in my early forties. Maybe it's time that I get serious about finding my special person.

I always thought it would happen naturally. That when I found the one, I'd know it. That's how it was for my best friends. Just because it went that way for them doesn't mean it will for me, though. If I don't do something about it, I'm going to end up old and lonely, and my balls might actually end up falling off. I can't let that happen. I like my balls.

That only means one thing, I guess. I need to start looking for my Little girl.

"WAIT, can we sit at that table over there?"

I glance at my date, the hair on the back of my neck prickling. From the moment I picked her up, I've been ready to take her home again. Why the fuck did I think trying to date was a good idea? It's a terrible fucking idea. The worst. This is a huge mistake.

The hostess glances at me for permission, but I give a slight shake of my head. "Take us to our reserved table."

Sharleen, my date and pain in the ass for the

evening, lets out a whine of protest that sounds like nails on a chalkboard. "I want to sit out here, where we can see people and they can see us."

Of course she does. She wants everyone who's anyone to see her with a billionaire so she can brag about it to all her friends. This date is nothing more than a way to gain clout within her social circle. I may not be a celebrity, but I'm well known in the community of wealth in Seattle. So are Declan, Killian, Bash, Kieran, and Ronan. For many reasons.

I met Sharleen a year or so ago at a party. She seemed cool, non-clingy, and like she had her shit together. Then we ran into each other again recently at Chloe and the other girls' influencer launch party for their makeup line. Again, she seemed cool. But after catching up in the car tonight on the way to the restaurant, I realized I'd been fooled. She's already talking about going to the Caribbean together. On my dime, of course.

"We're going to the table in the back. It's quieter and safer," I say dryly.

From the way her eyes bulge, it's obvious she hadn't thought about the potential danger of being with me. Being in the mob isn't all fun and games. We're always on edge. Always ready for danger.

As soon as we're seated, she snaps her fingers at the hostess. "I'd like a Cosmopolitan."

Running my tongue over my teeth, I force myself to

stay quiet. If she were my girl talking to someone like that, I'd haul her ass into the bathroom and spank her until she was sorry and regretful. But she's not mine and she never will be. Not in this lifetime and not in the next, either.

I offer a tight smile to the hostess as an apology before she scurries away, leaving me alone with this awful person.

"So, do you live in a penthouse around here? Maybe somewhere close?" She rubs her foot up my calf, and my stomach revolts. That's what she wants to know? If I live in a penthouse?

My neck is so tight it's painful. This was a huge mistake. I can't believe I did this. All because Cali was worried about me not dating and wanted to set me up on a dating site. I'm almost regretting not letting her do it because I'd bet a million dollars that whatever date Cali would arrange for me would be more enjoyable than this.

"No penthouse." I sit back and cross my arms over my chest.

Her shoulders drop, and she pops her lip out in a forced pout that isn't the least bit cute. "Oh. Well, a mansion, then?"

Fuck, it's going to be a long night.

2
KATIE

"Thank you so much!" I hand the iced, nine-pump caramel, three-pump vanilla, two-and-a-half espresso shots with whipped cream latte to the waiting customer. She should have just ordered a cup of pure sugar because that's basically what it is.

I'm all about sweet things. My hips are proof of that, but there is a line. Nine pumps of caramel in a single cup of coffee is way over it. Who am I to judge, though? That lady's daily coffee habit helps keep me afloat, so maybe I should start asking if she wants to add even more flavors to her order. Upsell and all.

When I look around the cozy shop, my shoulders relax. There are still a few people seated at tables, having their afternoon drink of choice while they do whatever it is they're doing. Enjoying their lives and taking a calm moment to breathe. It's heartwarming that they choose to come here. Most of them are regulars I see at least a few times a week. At least, I do now that I'm working more shifts.

Maybe I should have hired another employee after my last one left. At the time, the distraction of working more was nice, but now that one of my other employees needs time off to get ready for her college finals, I'm working a bit more than I'd like. It's a good thing I love my job. Some might feel like making coffee for a living isn't a career, but it is for me. This shop was my parents' dream, and now it's mine to keep alive.

I glance up at the clock and push myself back from the counter. Enough daydreaming. If I don't start my closing duties now, I won't get out of here on time, and I've been here since five this morning. My bed is calling my name. After I head to my parents' house to get some more packing done.

For the next half hour, I clean the espresso machine until it's back to the glistening chrome it should be. Soft pop and country play over the speakers, and I end up humming along quietly as I work. One by one, customers leave, and the shop empties.

I start grinding coffee beans for tomorrow morning when the door chimes. After switching off the machine, I turn to meet the new customer at the register but when I see who it is, I practically run around to the front of the shop.

"Chloe!" We swing our arms around each other and hug. Then I realize she's not here alone. She's with another woman, and there's a large, terrifying man lurking near the entrance with his eyes glued to them.

Chloe grins, her eyes sparkling. She's so happy it's vibrating off her. I'm thrilled she found Bash. I don't know much about him other than what she's told me.

"Hi! How are you? I've missed you," she squeals. "Oh, this is my sister-in-law, Cali." Chloe motions to the woman, then points toward the man. "That's Patrick. He's our chauffeur for today."

When I peer back at him, I shrink under the glare he shoots our way.

"Not your chauffeur," he mumbles.

Cali waves her hand dismissively. "He's a bit sour about it. Don't mind him. I love this shop!"

She walks around, looking at the various displays of gifts we sell. I turn my attention back to Chloe, my tummy doing a weird flutter.

"What are you doing here? Want me to make you your favorite drink?"

"As much as I'd love that, if I have caffeine this late in the day, I'll be up all night driving Bash up the wall." Chloe giggles and shifts from foot to foot for a second. "I just came to see how you were. We were in the neighborhood, so I made Patrick stop. How have you been?"

My heart squeezes as sadness settles over me. I

know Chloe is asking from a genuinely caring place, but I hate the question. Is there a right answer? I don't feel like there is. "I'm okay. Still working on clearing out my parents' house. I need to get it up for sale soon. I can't afford to keep paying the mortgage."

Chloe brings her hand to her chest and steps forward, wrapping me up into another hug. "Is there anything I can do? Me and my friends can come help. You'd love them, and they'd totally love you."

I hug her back and let myself find comfort in her arms. "Thank you for offering. I'm close to being done. I've been going there every night after work for a bit, and I think I only have a few more trips before the realtor can step in."

She holds on for a long moment before she releases me and steps back with tears in her eyes. My mom always loved Chloe, and Chloe was always offering to help when her cancer returned.

I squeeze her arms. "I'm okay. I promise. Honestly, I'm ready to put all of this behind me and move on. Maybe make some friends or find a hobby or date. If I can ever find the time," I huff and wave my hand dismissively. "I'm getting tired of only getting action from my smutty books."

We burst out giggling. It's nice to laugh. I haven't been doing enough of it. Chloe suddenly stills, her eyes darting to mine and then toward Cali before her mouth curls into a smile. "Yeah, you definitely should date.

Find yourself a hot man with money who will sweep you off your feet."

Shaking my head, I scoff. "I don't need a man with money. Just someone loyal and funny. If he knows how to make me scream, that'd be a plus."

Cali walks up as I finish and grabs onto Chloe's forearm. "Oh my God," she murmurs.

"Uh-huh," Chloe replies.

I glance back and forth between the women. "I'm confused. What?"

Chloe shakes her head. "Oh, it's nothing. Dating sounds fun, though! Do you have any prospects in mind?"

Well, yeah. Thor, my vibrator, but I'm not going to tell them that. "No. Not at all. I guess I'll have to join one of those dating sites or something. I've heard some pretty sketchy stories about them, though. I've never really had time for relationships. I'm not even sure how to go about finding a boyfriend."

Cali and Chloe glance at each other, smirking.

"Sometimes, relationships just fall right into your lap. I guess when the right person comes along, it'll just happen naturally," Cali says, looking down at her hot pink fingernails.

I shrug. "I guess. I don't know. I'll figure it out when the time comes. First, I need to get my parents' house sold and find more hours in the day." Because seriously, I don't have the time for a man. I barely have time to make a decent meal before I fall asleep for a few hours. And then I start all over the next morning.

"If you decide you want our help, we'd be happy to. But either way, let's keep in touch more. As soon as things slow down for you, let's do the girls' night we've always talked about." Chloe reaches out and grabs my hand, and a swell of emotion runs through me.

"I'd really love that. Thank you." I pull her in for another hug, a brief one this time, before smiling at Cali. The woman doesn't hesitate to grab me and throw her arms around me, catching me by surprise.

"It was so nice to meet you," Cali squeals excitedly when she steps back. "Chloe has said the sweetest things about you."

Gosh, I might be in tears by the time they leave. Are women always this supportive of each other? I don't have a lot of experience with friendships, so I'm not really sure.

"I'll text you in the next day or two, and we'll plan something," Chloe says as they make their way toward the exit.

The large, terrifying man gives me a stiff smile before he opens the door for them.

"Okay. Sounds great. I'm so glad you stopped by," I tell them. They head toward a pristine, sleek black Escalade. "Nice meeting you, Cali!"

"Nice meeting you, too! Can't wait to see you again soon. It's going to be great. So great!" She waves enthusiastically, leaving me staring in confusion. What's going to be great? Did I miss something?

They drive away, and just as I'm about to turn the lock on the door, Tom peers through the glass. I wave him in.

"Hi, Tom! I was about to dump the coffee carafes, so you made it just in time. I have some leftover pastries for you, too."

They're actually extras I make just for him, but I don't tell him that. Tom has been coming to the shop for as long as I can remember. He's homeless and pushes a cart around with all of his belongings in. Even though I've told him he can, he never comes in if there are customers. He doesn't show up until just before closing when I'm about to dump the carafes.

"How're you doing?" I round the counter and fill a cup for him.

"Cold today. Feels like it could snow."

I frown and glance out the large windows surrounding the shop. We don't get a ton of snow in Seattle, so when we do, it shuts the city down.

"You think it's going to snow this late in the season?" I ask.

Somehow, Tom always calls the weather correctly. Maybe it's because he lives out in the elements, so he feels it when things change. Whatever it is, I trust his forecast more than the weather people. But snow? I'm not so sure about that.

"Think so. Maybe a few inches," he replies, running his hand over his scruffy beard.

I slide his coffee across the counter and sigh. "You need to go to a shelter if it gets that cold. Or you could take me up on my offer to sleep in the back office."

He brings the cup to his lips and takes a long drink, ignoring my comment like he always does. "Thanks, Katie-girl. Stay safe, Little one. Lock this door behind me."

Then he heads back outside, giving me one last wave before he disappears to wherever it is he goes. I'm not sure when or why my parents decided to start giving him free coffee. All I know is that my dad really respected Tom, and my mom doted on him every time she saw him. Whatever the reason, I'll continue honoring that until he stops coming. As much as I hate to admit it, it makes my heart ache to know that one day he won't be here anymore. I guess, in a way, he's one of the few people I consider a friend. Maybe even family.

Although, after today, I think that might change. I might be in my mid-twenties, but I can hardly wait for a girls' night.

3
GRADY

"**G**rady..."

Glancing up from my disassembled pistol, I raise an eyebrow at Chloe. She's not usually one to seek me out. Especially in the armory.

"What's up, Little one? You come down here to learn to shoot?"

She eyes the gun I'm in the process of cleaning and shrugs. "Maybe another day. I was actually wondering if you would go with me to pick out a gift for Daddy."

I'm not sure why she's asking me for help. Her brother is Bash's best friend, and Declan and Ronan are his brothers. Granted, I *am* their cousin. I'm closer to Ronan than I am to Bash.

"Kieran probably knows what he likes better than I

would. Or ask Ronan. If you ask me, I'd say get him some itching powder."

Her eyes narrow as she wanders in closer. "Yeah, but Kieran is busy, and Ronan left for Ireland this morning. And itching powder is mean. Don't be a bully, Grady. Besides, surely you can help pick out a decent watch. I don't know anything about men's timepieces, and you love them."

I do love a good quality, expensive watch. Especially when I'm about to kill someone; I make a show of checking my wrist before I tell them it's time to die. Maybe I'll keep that to myself, though. No need to scare Chloe.

"You need to go right now?" I ask as I start wiping down the metal frame. Clearly, she can see I'm in the middle of something. Her chin drops with determination, and I already know she's not giving up on this.

"Yes. I want to do something nice for him because he's always doing such sweet things for me."

I'm sure he'd find a blowjob to be much nicer than a new watch, but I'm not going to tell her that either. Bash might murder me if I talked about anything sexual with his girl. He's the most possessive bastard I've ever met. And I'm jealous as fuck of him. Ever since he got with Chloe, the idiot walks around with a perma-grin on his face like he won the fucking lottery. I guess, in a way, he did.

"Fine. Let me reassemble my gun, and then we'll go."

Bouncing up and down on her tiptoes, she claps her hands. "Yay! Thank you. Cali's coming too."

Awesome. So I'm going to have two brats ganging up on me this afternoon. Chloe is mostly a sweetheart, but anytime Cali is around, there's some kind of naughtiness that happens. She's pure trouble. Hell, for all I know, there's a dating profile out there for me somewhere that she's created. I should probably look into it and make sure that isn't the case.

As soon as Chloe disappears, I put my Glock back together like a puzzle I've already done a million times and chamber a bullet before I tuck it into my shoulder holster. I send a text to Cullen, one of our main bodyguards and drivers, telling him to have a car out front for us. Then I send a message to the group we have set up between the top six.

Grady: *I've been summoned by Chloe and Cali to take them shopping. Declan, Bash, are you aware of this?*

Ronan: *Better you than me. I'll pray for you, bro.*

Grady: *Why the fuck are you going to Ireland again? This is the third time in two months.*

Sarcastic asshole.

Declan: *Cali let me know. I told her it was fine as long as you didn't mind.*

Grady: *As if we ever get a choice when it comes to these brats?*

Bash: *Choice? Fuck no. That went out the window when we said I do. They just want to spend some quality time with you.*

Doubtful, but if Chloe is wanting to shop for a gift for Bash, she may have fed him that line of BS.

Grady: *Quality time, my ass. I'll be lucky if I make it back alive. Cullen's driving, so I can drink the entire time.*

Killian: *Good luck with them. Scarlet wanted to go too, but I made her take a nap because she was being a bit too sassy. You can thank me now.*

Grady: *Gee. Thanks.*

Kieran: *Our girls are angels. Quit bitching about having to spend time with them.*

Declan: *Love seeing Kieran become a big fucking marshmallow since he married Paisley. Angels? That's a stretch.*

Grady: *None of you are helpful. I'll be back later. If we're not back by five, send help.*

Ronan: *(laughing emoji)*

Grady: *Not going to answer my question about why you're going to Ireland, huh?*

Bash: *Be careful with them. They might be brats, but they're our everything.*

My heartbeat quickens, and an emptiness settles in the pit of my stomach. I've never been a jealous person, but lately, it's been hitting me hard.

Grady: *I'd die before I let anything happen to them.*

I mean that with my entire soul. I would do anything to keep them safe. Hell, I've taken a bullet trying to protect them. I'd do it again, too. They're my family just as much as the mafia.

Before I close my messenger app, I delete several messages that Sharleen sent over the past few hours. The woman isn't giving up, no matter how much I ignore her calls and texts.

Chloe and Cali are waiting for me in the foyer. As soon as I enter, they go quiet.

Narrowing my gaze, I look between them. "What are you two plotting?"

They look at each other with doll-like innocent eyes before they turn back to me.

"We're not plotting anything, silly. Sheesh. So paranoid. You ready to go?" Chloe asks, skipping toward the front door.

Cullen has the Escalade out front and stands at the rear door, holding it open for us. Once the girls are loaded into the back, I get into the passenger seat and grab the bottle of Jameson from the side compartment.

"You probably need that to deal with those two," Cullen says as he shifts into drive.

"Aye. I have no clue what I've gotten myself into. Suppose I'll find out when we get there," I reply.

The women chatter non-stop in the back while we pass through the city streets toward the address Chloe gave us.

We're only a few minutes away when Chloe leans forward and taps me on the shoulder. "Oh, can we stop and get a coffee first? The shop I used to work at is just two blocks away. I'm dying for a praline latte."

Jesus Christ. "Do you really think caffeine this late in the day is a good idea?"

She shrugs. "I'll get decaf. I mostly just want it because it's so yummy. Please, Grady? It's right on the way."

I glance toward Cullen who smirks as he keeps his eyes on the road. Bastard. He's not going to help me out at all with them.

"Fine. Where is it?"

Two turns later, we're pulling into the parking lot of a plaza with several stores, including the coffee shop at the end named Twisted Bean. Kind of a clever name, actually.

Cullen stops right in front of the storefront, not bothering to find a parking space. We don't live by the rules. Wherever we go, we do what we want, and the people around us adjust whether they like it or not.

As soon as I step out into the dreary, overcast weather, the back door swings open and Cali hops out. Clenching my jaw, I step in front of her, blocking her between the door and the car.

"Are you supposed to freely get out of a car?" I raise an eyebrow and wait.

Cali swallows as she looks up at me. It's rare that I truly get stern with any of the girls, but when it comes to their safety, I don't fuck around. I will put her ass right back into the car and make Cullen drive us home if she gives me any sass about it.

"Sorry, Grady," she murmurs. "I was excited and forgot."

I keep her pinned with my gaze. "What are you so excited about? It's just coffee. Do it again, and our outing will end early. Understand?"

She bobs her head and bites her lip, her eyes downcast. "Yes, sir."

Aw, fuck. I didn't mean to make her feel bad.

Using my index finger, I hook it under her chin to tip her head back. "I only want to keep you girls safe. Okay? Believe it or not, I love you brats."

She beams at me again and throws her arms around my neck. "I know. We love you, too."

When I finally move out of her way, she steps to the side, and I hold out my hand to help Chloe out of the car. She's not as used to seeing my stern side. She's also not as sassy as Cali, so she doesn't say anything other than a quick thank you as she slides out. I give her hand a reassuring squeeze before I let go, and she shoots me a sweet smile that melts me inside.

As we enter the shop, a bell overhead rings. I look around, taking in our surroundings like I always do. Floor-to-ceiling windows let in a ton of light, making it warm and welcoming. It's also larger than I expected. The space is slightly narrow but long, with bathrooms at the very back. There's lots of seating, both tables and chairs and couches set up in clusters. Soft music plays in the background. This is a coffee shop I could enjoy coming to—unlike those wildly busy corporate ones that overcharge and don't even fill the entire cup.

"Welcome to Twisted Bean!" My cock jumps as the sweet, melodic voice floats through the air and hits me like a brick to the head. Goosebumps cover my skin, and I can't breathe. My gaze darts around the space again, desperately looking for the woman who spoke, but I can't find her. I stride forward, searching in panic.

Everything around me disappears, and the only thing I can focus on is that sweet sound. Where is she? Who is she? That's a silly fucking question. She's mine. I know it without even laying eyes on her. I know it without knowing a single thing about her. She could be married for all I know. It doesn't matter. *She's mine.*

When I get midway down the long counter, a small woman steps out from behind the tall espresso machine. She raises her gaze to me, blinking several times before her plush lips fall open. I can't help but stare, mesmerized by everything about her.

A flush blooms on her cheeks as she raises her gaze to me. "H-hi. Um, hi. Welcome to Twisted Bean. What can I get for you?" She runs her fingers over some of the loose hairs that have fallen from her ponytail and tucks them behind her ear, her hand trembling.

I take my time taking her in. Silky, caramel brown hair pulled up in a high ponytail with a pale pink velvet scrunchy. Round blue eyes with the longest lashes I've ever seen. The high counter blocks most of her body, but she's definitely curvy. My girl likes to eat. And that makes me so damn happy. I can't wait to feed her. And feast *on* her.

"Katie!" Chloe skips up from behind and waves at my woman. Katie. It's adorable. Just like her.

Katie's attention slowly shifts from me to Chloe and Cali. I don't like it. I want her eyes on me. Always on me and no one else. Holy fuck. What's wrong with me? I've never reacted to a woman like this. Never felt this kind of all-consuming possessiveness. It's uncomfortable and addicting at the same time.

"Hi!" Katie squeals and then scurries around from behind the counter toward us.

Holy fuck, she's perfect.

Wide, round hips, a soft tummy, big tits, and thick thighs that I want to worship. Jesus. God was feeling generous when he made her.

Katie and Chloe hug tightly before Cali takes her turn. When they pull away, Katie peeks up at me and swallows. "This must be Bash?" she asks, disappointment in her voice.

Chloe and Cali burst out laughing. What the fuck is so funny?

"Oh, goodness, no. This is Grady. He works with Bash and Cali's husband, Declan. Grady, this is Katie.

She owns Twisted Bean," Chloe says, motioning toward Katie.

I gawk unapologetically, memorizing everything I can about her. "Nice to meet you, Katie." I stick out my hand to shake hers, my heart pounding as she glances down at my tattoo-covered fingers, her tongue popping out to wet her lips. She doesn't look like someone who dates men covered in ink. Or men who work for criminal empires. That's about to change, though. Her entire life is about to be turned upside down, and so is mine. I can feel it.

The second she slides her fingers into my palm, my cock grows painfully hard, and every hair on my body stands on end.

"Nice to meet you," she replies quietly.

I keep hold of her hand for longer than is acceptable, but I can't seem to let go. When she finally tugs it free, an emptiness settles inside me. She's meant to be touching me. Only me.

She pulls her bottom lip between her teeth and turns toward Chloe. "Do you want coffee?"

Chloe grins. "You know it."

My eyes go directly to Katie's ass when she turns around. The skinny jeans she has on hug her like a glove, giving me the perfect view. Cali snorts beside me, breaking my attention away. When I look down at her, she waggles her eyebrows and then points toward Katie.

"Hush," I scold quietly.

Her knowing grin irritates me. Why do I have a feeling this was a set-up?

"Can I get you something?" Katie asks me when she's back behind the counter.

Her voice is sweet like honey and has an innocence about it when she talks. Everything about her seems innocent.

I study her as I run a hand over my beard. Would it be too much to ask her to sit on my face? Because that's something I'd like her to get me. Probably not appropriate for a first-time meet, so I smile. "Make me whatever you want, and I'll drink it."

Pink blotches appear on her cheeks, and she quickly lowers her gaze for a second and then looks at Cali. She fidgets nervously with a cup, and I want to grab hold of her to soothe her nerves. I'm used to people being nervous around me, but she has no reason to be.

"I'll have whatever Chloe's having," Cali announces before she wanders off toward one of the gift displays. Chloe quickly follows, leaving me alone with Katie. I can't take my eyes off her. I have so many questions. Ones I definitely won't get answers to right now, but hopefully soon.

She moves behind the espresso machine, but I can still watch her from this angle as she prepares three drinks with such precision that I'd bet she could do it with her eyes closed. Every so often, she peers at me and then quickly looks away when she realizes I'm staring at her.

"Do you like your coffee sweet?" she asks quietly, almost timidly.

Fuck no. "If you like it, I'll like it." The only thing I want that's sweet is my mouth on her pussy, but I'll drink whatever she gives me just to make her happy.

The pink blotches appear again, and I'm quickly becoming addicted to seeing them. I want to see her lower set of cheeks pink from my handprint.

She spends the next couple of minutes pouring and mixing, and I watch every movement. After she fills a small metal pitcher and starts steaming it, she glances at me again, holding my gaze for several seconds. All of a sudden, the milk boils over onto her hand, and she jumps back with a hiss, dropping the pitcher.

"Ouch!" she cries, yanking her hand to her chest.

I race behind the counter and grab her wrist, tugging her toward the sink.

"I'm okay," she says tightly. "It happens sometimes."

That's not acceptable. But I'll deal with that later. Right now, she needs cold water. I turn on the tap and gently move her hand under the stream. When she lets out a quiet wince, I growl.

"I'm fine." She turns her pained, cornflower-blue eyes up to me, and I want to scold her for lying to me.

Ignoring that thought, I hold her wrist firmly. Cali and Chloe appear beside us.

"Ouch. I hated when that happened," Chloe comments.

"It happens a lot?" I demand, frowning at her.

Chloe shrinks back slightly. "Not a lot."

Katie tries to pull her hand free. "I'm fine. It doesn't hurt anymore. Really, I'm good."

Reluctantly, I release her and grab a towel to dry her off. She tries to take it from me, but I don't let her.

All three women stare at me as I gently pat her skin dry. The silence is awkward between us, but I don't give a shit. When I'm satisfied that she's not going to blister, I let go of her and sigh. "You need some cooling ointment for it."

Katie peers up at me, her chest rising and falling quickly. Good. I'm having an effect on her, too. It's not only one-sided. Thank fuck for that. I wonder if I reached between her legs if her panties would be wet. The way she keeps shifting her legs together, I'm thinking they would be.

"Um, okay? It's really fine. I do that at least once a day. I need to get the steamer fixed. It's blowing too hard. I just haven't had time to schedule anything." She smiles nervously, waving her hand like it's no big deal.

Cali rolls her eyes. "Grady is a bit overprotective. Then again, all of our men are. You'll get used to it."

Yep, this was definitely a fucking set-up. Those

little brats. I'm going to hug both of them for it later. After I lecture them. Then I'm going to take them to Build-A-Bear and let them get whatever they want. And when we get home, I'm going to tell their Daddies about the sneaky shit they did.

Chloe moves over to the coffees that Katie was preparing and takes over like she still works here. "What time are you off today? Why don't you come over for dinner? You need to meet Bash, and you can also meet Scarlet and Paisley. We could have an impromptu movie night afterward."

My heart leaps in my chest at the thought of Katie coming to dinner. Chloe is definitely getting a reward after we leave. I'd prefer it if Katie came to my house to eat. Alone. But I'll take what I can get. I am a complete stranger, after all. I won't be for long. Just because I know she's mine doesn't mean she does.

"Oh, um, I can't."

Fuck. I don't like that answer. Why can't she? Does she have a man she has to go home to? I'll kill him. She'd probably get over it in a few months before she's ready to move on to me. I can wait it out.

She shifts from one foot to the other. "I'm meeting with the realtor tonight. He wants me to make some improvements to my parents' house before I put it on the market, so we're meeting to go over his suggestions to see what I can afford to do."

I don't like anything she just said. He? Who the hell

is he? She's going to be alone with this realtor? Selling her parents' house? What she can afford? She shouldn't be worrying about that. She should never have to worry about money or affording anything. That's my job. The only thing she needs to be concerned about is being Daddy's good girl.

Chloe's shoulders drop, but she nods. "Tomorrow night?"

Katie purses her lips for a second, her eyes flicking to mine and then back to Chloe. "I might be able to do that. I'll text you later to let you know for sure."

Fuck. I don't think I can wait twenty-four hours to see her again. How did I go from being completely single to thinking about what my wedding vows to this woman will be?

4
KATIE

Holy espresso beans.

I think I orgasmed a little when he touched me.

This man is making me forget what words are. Do I even remember what my name is right now? How can one person be so gorgeous, mysterious, terrifying, and kind-looking all at the same time? I'm not sure how, but Grady pulls it off.

When he first came in, and I had to keep looking higher and higher just to meet his eyes, I was breathless. He's got to be at least six-four. And dressed in a black suit that definitely isn't off the rack. I almost wondered if he was a model. Then he held out his tattooed fingers, and I was surprised. He must be covered in them.

Then, after stumbling over my words, I burned

myself with the stupid steamer that I've been meaning to have fixed for months. Now I'm thoroughly embarrassed and wish the ground would swallow me up whole. My skin still tingles from the pain, but I don't want him to know that because he seems a bit pissed off over it happening. It was pretty hot the way he got all over-the-top protective.

Chloe keeps catching my eye, tilting her head toward Grady, her mouth tipped into a half-smirk. He won't stop staring at me like I'm the most interesting thing he's ever seen. It's unnerving. I look like a train wreck, and I might even smell of BO right now, so I don't know what he finds so interesting. Plus, I'm me, and he's him. We are definitely *not* on the same level. Literally and figuratively.

Yet despite all that, my vagina loves every second of the attention. My breasts, too. They're aching, desperate for just a whisper of a touch from him. A girl can dream.

It's obvious he's rich. Not to mention hot. And charming. The way he took control when I hurt myself was swoon-worthy. He was gentle but stern at the same time. I'm not used to that kind of treatment. I'm used to being the one taking care of others. I've spent the better part of my life doing so.

Needing to get away from Grady's intensity, I help Chloe finish the drinks, topping them with whipped cream. After I put the lid on Grady's cup, I hold my breath and hold it out for him.

"It's a light roast pour-over with steamed milk, a splash of Irish cream, and whipped cream. It's my favorite." As I speak, he studies me, bringing the cup up to his nose to sniff it.

"It's your favorite?" he asks before he takes a drink.

He has a slight accent when he talks, which only adds to his appeal. It's so light that I can't tell where it might originate from, though.

I nod as he swallows, his Adam's apple bobbing. Who knew an act so simple could ignite my body like wildfire? Thank goodness I wore a bra with a little padding today because otherwise, he'd get a nice view of my budded nipples.

"Aye," he says. "Just became my favorite, too. Thanks, lass. See you tomorrow."

Oh my God. It's an Irish accent. I think I've died and gone to heaven. I can hardly wait to get home so I can load my e-reader with a bunch of Irish mafia books because he totally gives off that vibe. Although he's so tall and fit he could be a sports player. Ohhh, maybe he's a hockey player. That would be hot. Is Irish hockey a thing?

Then he puts a hundred-dollar bill on the counter and strides toward the door, leaving me, Cali, and Chloe staring at his backside. Damn, the man sure fills out a suit. His trousers are molded perfectly to his ass, giving me the best exit view. Definitely a hockey player.

"What just happened?" I murmur.

Chloe nudges me and wraps her arm around my waist. "I think he just fell in love. Text me later. Good luck with the real estate agent."

She leans in and gives me a quick kiss on the cheek before she grabs their beverages, and they follow Grady outside.

I blink several times as her words finally start to register. Did she just say…? No. I misheard her. I must have. There's no way she said what I think she did. Obviously, I'm so tired that I'm delusional. Delusional and unexpectedly horny.

I don't have a ton of experience with men. I'm certainly not a virgin, but my body has never had such a reaction to anyone before. If only a man like him could ever love a woman like me. He probably has supermodels throwing themselves at him on a regular basis. Not that I blame them. I don't know how Chloe and Cali act so nonchalantly around him. I could barely breathe the entire time he was here.

What would it be like to be with a man like that? I bet he knows what to do to make a woman feel good.

As far-fetched as it may be that Grady would ever be interested in me, I'm sure going to enjoy fantasizing about him tonight when I'm tucked in. Bedtime can't come soon enough.

Keeping Katie

My stomach twists. I'm going to be sick if I don't calm down. How am I supposed to do that, though? The improvements the realtor suggested will cost me over twenty thousand dollars. Do I look like I'm rolling in money? My savings account is about as sad as Eeyore on a rainy day, and that's pretty pitiful. I'm barely staying above water. Thankfully, my parents' health insurance company has been waiting for their payment until I sell the house. They're losing patience, though, and have started making threats that I can't even think about. I cannot and will not lose the shop. I just hope the money from the sale will cover everything.

"I'll have to think about this. Maybe I can manage a few of these." I glance at the paper Calvin gave me. "I could paint the walls myself. That's easy enough. And I could fix the gate, probably."

Calvin smiles and leans against the kitchen island, his gaze raking down my body and back up again. "It's up to you, doll. Just remember that the selling price will be based on the improvements you make. If buyers see a lot of stuff to do, they'll have leverage to offer less. I'm only trying to help you out."

Right. So, either way, I'm screwed. None of this

would be happening if it weren't for the stupid life insurance company that dropped my mom's coverage a few months before she died. The worst part is, I didn't know until after she was gone, and I'd reached out for the policy payout. Now, I'm left with no choice but to sell their house to pay off their medical debts.

After searching for realtors, I somehow ended up with Calvin. And honestly, I'm not a fan of him. I've never sold or bought a house, though, so I don't know if this is normal or not. I have a feeling he calls everyone by some kind of nickname, but it feels slimy every time he calls me doll. Slimy, just like his overly gelled hair. Barf.

Once he leaves, after giving me an awkward half-hug that caught me off guard, I get to work and load a few boxes into my car. I'd like to say this house means something to me, but I've spent more time at Twisted Bean and at the hospital since I was a kid. The coffee shop is more my home than this house. I think my parents felt that way, too. We made so many memories there. Ones I'll cherish forever.

It's way past sunset by the time I lock the front door, yawning as I do. As I drive away, I glance over my shoulder. There's a black Escalade parked along the curb a few houses down. It's similar to the one Chloe came to the shop in. The one she rode in with Grady. I squint harder to see if I recognize it. Wow. I shake my head and laugh out loud. I must really be losing it. As if he would follow me to my parents' house after meeting me one time. Good lord. I've been reading way too many stalker romances.

Will he be at dinner if I go? He made it seem like he would be there. I'm not sure if that makes it better. I was barely functional around him today. He's probably used to that. I'm sure women lose their ability to talk around him all the time.

My shoulders slump. I can't go to dinner tomorrow as much as I want to. The list I have is so long, I'll be busy for days. Hopefully, Chloe will take a raincheck. Once again, my responsibilities outweigh a chance at fun.

By the time I get home, my mind is made up, even though I wish I could change it. I send Chloe a text, letting her know I can't make it to dinner because of all the things I need to do. A girls' night sounds fun and exactly what I need, but the house is the priority.

Chloe: *Let's plan for this weekend, then? You've got to eat sometime.*

I smile, my heart feeling a bit lighter.

Katie: *Yes, I suppose you're right. This weekend works.*

That gives me four days to work on the house. I'm sure I can get a ton accomplished by then.

Birds chirp happily as I unlock the front door to the shop. Why are they so glad to be awake this early? It's pure torture, if you ask me. Especially since I only got a few hours of sleep last night. Getting home late, thoughts about everything I need to do to my parents' house, then visions of the hot man who starred in all my fantasies last night—I'm a walking zombie today. Still, the orgasms were worth it.

Once inside, I lock the door behind me and get to work brewing the carafes of drip, starting up the espresso machine, and making sure we have enough cups and lids set out for the day.

Even though I hate waking up so early, I love this time of the morning. The world is still quiet while the sun slowly climbs out of its own bed and brightens the world. The windows allow me to watch as things come to life. It's the most Zen part of my day because my thoughts are still sleeping until I've had my first hit of coffee.

The bookstore owner next door knocks on one of the front windows as she passes by. I wave at her and smile. It's our usual morning greeting to each other. A small thing that gives me a sense of normalcy. I can't remember the last time my life felt that way.

Right at five o'clock, I turn on the neon open sign and unlock the door. My morning shift employee won't be here until six since the rush doesn't typically start until after then anyway. I get the first hour to slowly get into my groove with a few regular customers who come in on their way to work.

Before I make it back behind the counter, the door chime rings. I pause mid-step, caught off guard by the immediate customer. Usually, I'm able to get my own coffee made before I have to make someone else's. Guess I'll have to wait a little longer this morning. I turn to greet whoever it is but immediately freeze.

Swallowing, I stare at Grady in stunned silence. It takes a second for me to get my shit together and force a tight smile. A flush starts at my cheeks and works its way down my entire body, right to my clit. I might be a zombie this morning, but my pussy is wide awake and purring like a cat in heat. My gaze wanders behind him, waiting for Chloe to appear, but she doesn't. It's only him. "Um, good morning. Welcome to Twisted Bean."

Even at this hour, he's dressed in a crisp black suit; only this time, he has on a long jacket to match, black leather gloves, and a dark gray scarf. He looks edible. And way more awake than me.

Crap.

Did I put on concealer this morning? Nope. I sure didn't. At least I brushed my hair and put on deodorant.

"Good morning, lass," Grady says with a half-smirk. "Cold out there. Hope you were bundled up when you came in."

I shudder, my skin prickling. That's sweet of him to care. Although I'm certainly not going to tell him I was not, in fact, bundled up in more than a jean jacket because I was in such a hurry.

What is he doing here? It's barely daylight out.

"Did you lose something yesterday?" I ask, looking around the shop as if something is going to jump out at me.

"No, lass. Think I found something, though."

My head snaps up, and I meet his gaze. His eyes are practically glowing. A mix of green, gold, and blue. Penetrating to the point I almost feel naked. Exposed. Can he see all my insecurities? My flaws?

"Was hoping I could get another one of those coffees you made me," he adds.

Oh, right. Duh. That's why he's here. He wants coffee. Silly me.

I stride around the counter and grab a cup, nodding. "Of course. Coming right up."

He doesn't reply. Instead, he stares, watching me like a hawk as I make his beverage. This time, I keep my eyes on the task so I don't end up embarrassing myself again. It's not until I put a lid on the drink that he finally looks away.

"Here you go."

"Can I get a pastry too? Pick one you like."

My tummy does a little flutter. We stare at each other for a second. A shudder runs through me. I'm sure my cheeks would be bright pink if I looked in the mirror right now. Who needs a coat when he's around? Not me.

I reach into the glass case and pull out an apple strudel croissant. "Do you want it for here or to go?"

Why did I ask that? Obviously, he's not going to stay. He's not the kind of guy to spend his time in a coffee shop. Especially at five in the morning.

"For here." His voice is deep and velvety. A mix of harsh and smooth. There's a hint of sternness when he speaks that makes me want to immediately obey his every command.

"Okay. I'll heat it and bring it out to you," I offer.

He nods and drops a hundred-dollar bill on the counter near the cash register, then turns and sits at the table closest to me. Close enough that his rich, amber scent wafts through the air.

Last night, I fought the urge to text Chloe some more and ask her about Grady. Who he is. What he does. What kind of person he is. Based on how he carries himself, he's definitely in a position of power. Men don't walk around with his level of confidence unless they have a reason to. And while he seems kind enough, the tattoos on his hands, all the way down to his fingertips, cause a yellow caution flag to pop up in my mind. If this were one of the books I like to read, I'd say he's in the mafia, but this isn't a book. It's real life, and stuff like that isn't real.

As I pass the register to take him the pastry, I swipe the money he left on the counter and set it down with the plate. "I'm not sure where you normally drink coffee, but at Twisted Bean, it doesn't cost a hundred dollars."

The corner of his mouth twitches as he looks me up at down. "Got a little sass in there. I like it. Take a bite."

His eyes lower to the pastry and then back to me as my mouth goes slack. "Oh, um, no, that's yours. And since you left so much money yesterday, this one and the next twenty are on the house."

"Did you eat breakfast?"

"What?"

He sits back in the chair, his hands folded between his thighs as he looks at me expectantly. Definitely a man in a position of power. Is it pathetic that I have an urge to kneel before him? I've never had this feeling before, but something about him does it to me. I'm sure it happens to most women he comes across.

"I asked if you ate breakfast."

Thankfully, the door chime interrupts us because I have a feeling Grady wouldn't approve of me not having eaten breakfast already. There was an underlying disappointment in his tone. Even I caught onto it, and I'm not always the most observant.

Spinning on my heel, I smile at my first regular of the day and go to make his coffee.

"Morning, Mark. Same thing?"

Mark nods and leans against the counter. He's not much of a morning person, so he doesn't expect me to do much talking, which is nice. While I work, though, I feel Grady's gaze on me. I don't think I've ever been watched so closely.

I cash out Mark, and as he leaves, another customer enters. That's how it goes for the next while, so I stay busy and away from Grady. The entire time, he tracks my movements. He also glares at every male customer I help, no matter how old they are. It sends a naughty thrill up my spine. Is he jealous? That's almost laughable.

Erin comes bouncing in at six and gets right to work. She's a good employee and loves her job, so it's a win-win. Movement out of the corner of my eye catches my attention, and when I glance that way, Grady taps the table with the tip of his index finger and then signals for me to come over.

Heat rushes right down to my pussy. Why does him calling me over turn me on? And why do I want to rush right over to him?

As I approach his table, he pushes the chair next to him out a few inches. Tilting my head, I smile, then lower myself to sit, partially wishing I hadn't. His scent is potent. I'm drawn to him. I want to scoot closer. Climb onto his powerful thighs and snuggle right into his chest.

What the hell is wrong with me? Oh my God. Where are these thoughts coming from? When did I become such a needy hussy?

"Eat," he commands softly, motioning to the untouched pastry.

Scrunching my face, I shake my head. "That's yours."

"I want you to eat it. You need a proper breakfast." He picks up the fork and cuts a piece off, then stabs it. When he raises it to my mouth to feed me, I stop breathing. I've surely died and gone to another dimension.

"How do you know I didn't already have breakfast?"

When he narrows his gaze and raises an eyebrow, I swallow heavily. Can he see right through me?

"Little one," he says quietly, though there's no missing the threat in his voice.

The last thing I want to do is disappoint him, but letting him feed me is too much, especially in the middle of *my* coffee shop. I take the fork from him, careful not to touch him in the process. He doesn't look happy but releases it and sits back again.

"Would you like another coffee?" I ask once I swallow.

"No," he answers simply. "You're coming to dinner tonight."

He says it as a statement, like the decision is already

made. I shake my head and cut off another piece of pastry when he points to it.

"No. I can't. I talked to Chloe. We've planned for another night later this week."

His jaw flexes, and he gestures to the plate again. I roll my eyes but take another bite, surprised by how hungry I am. Normally, I don't eat in the morning. Coffee is my go-to.

"That displeases me. Did you find out what improvements need to be done to your parents' house?"

I drop the fork with a clatter and start coughing. "That displeases you? What does that even mean?"

Who says 'displeases'?

"Exactly what it sounds like. I'm unhappy that you're not coming to dinner. You didn't answer my question."

What question? I can't keep track of anything that's happening right now. Chloe's words suddenly replay in my mind.

I think he just fell in love.

There's no freaking way Grady is at all interested in me. He's him, and I'm me. We exist on different planets. Also, we just met yesterday.

I don't even know his last name.

"It's O'Brien."

"Huh?" My head is spinning.

The corners of his mouth tip up into a breathtaking

smile. "You said you didn't know my last name. It's O'Brien."

Shit. Now, I'm talking out loud, and I didn't even realize it. I need to get away from him before I say something dumb.

"Nothing you say is dumb. You can say whatever you want to me. Ask whatever you want."

Holy espresso. I'm making the biggest fool of myself. I could blame it on lack of sleep, but admitting that he was part of the reason I didn't sleep is not on my list of things I want to do.

"I need to get back to work," I blurt as I jump up from the chair and rush behind the counter without a glance back.

I force myself not to look at him as I help Erin with the morning crowd. The next time I glance at the table, he's gone. I drop my shoulders as disappointment floods me.

When I go to clean the plate that still has the mostly uneaten pastry on it, I find the hundred-dollar bill I tried to give back to him and a note scribbled on the back of a business card with his name and number on it.

Be a good girl and eat it.

Plate in hand, I scurry back to my small office and pull out my phone to text Chloe.

Katie: *I think I'm in big, big trouble.*

Then I finish the delicious, mouthwatering pastry,

thinking about what a good girl I'm being the entire time.

I HAVE paint specks on my hands and arms, even though I scrubbed until my skin was raw in the shower this morning. It's probably pointless since I'll be doing the same thing tonight and will have a fresh set of spatters to wash off.

With a sigh, I turn on the open sign and unlock the door. When the door chimes before I make it behind the counter again, I stop mid-step. It can't be him. There's no way. It's only a coincidence that someone is here again within seconds of me opening.

"Morning, lass. You should always check to see who enters when you hear the door. Could be someone dangerous."

Oh, it's someone dangerous, all right.

When I turn, my breath hitches. His light brown hair is perfectly styled, but instead of being overly gelled, it looks touch-ably tousled. He has a different coat and scarf on, but from what I can tell, the suit is the same. Does he have a row of them in his closet? From its crispness, I doubt it's the same one he wore yesterday.

"Good morning," I say, barely above a whisper.

His smirk turns into a grin. "Cold out there. Colder than normal for this time of year. Make sure you wear a thick jacket whenever you go outside."

Why does that feel like a threat? Does he know I've only been wearing my favorite jean jacket?

"Um, do you want coffee?" I ask, my voice strangled.

"Aye. Same kind. And a pastry. You pick it."

I glance up at him, wanting to figure him out. I don't understand why he's here again. Twisted Bean is near and dear to my heart but it's not as if it's some magical place where a man like Grady O'Brien would want to hang out on the regular.

When I slide his cup across the counter, he sets down a hundred-dollar bill and returns to the same table as yesterday. My lips twitch as I go about warming his pastry. Surely, I'm not imagining this tension between us. I might not be as experienced as some women, but I can feel the pull between us. It's like a dance, but I don't know the steps.

"This is a cranberry pecan scone." After I set the plate in front of him, along with his money, I slowly start to back away.

"Did you make it, lass?"

"Yes. I make all the pastries. I have a full kitchen in the back."

He nods and slowly slides his gaze over me, his

tongue dipping out to wet his lips. It doesn't feel slimy like when Calvin does it. Instead, it feels like a gentle caress over my skin everywhere Grady looks.

"You were painting last night?"

I suck in a breath. How does he know that? Is that his black Escalade I keep seeing?

"You have paint on your hands," he adds.

Oh, duh. God, I'm losing it.

"Uh, yeah. I'm painting my parents' house so I can sell it."

He flexes his jaw and nods. "Busy girl. When do you find time to sleep?"

Warning flags fly high in my mind. This feels like a trap. But I'm not sure how or why.

"I don't need very much sleep," I reply, waving my hand dismissively.

The door chimes, and I'm once again pulled away from him, distracted by an ongoing string of customers. For the next hour, every time I glance up, his eyes are locked on me, tracking my every move. Then, he rises, and it's my turn to watch as he strides out of the shop, giving me an earth-shattering half-smile as he passes the counter. As soon as the door closes behind him, my heart sinks. I shouldn't miss a man I don't even know.

When I go to clean off his table, there's another of his business cards under the plate, along with the money.

Go to bed by nine at the latest and eat the scone.

And somehow, I find myself in my office, eating the scone while replaying our interaction in my mind. I'm also in bed by eight-thirty.

THIS TIME, when the door chimes right after I turn on the open sign, a smile touches my lips. I don't have to turn around to know it's Grady. It's almost as if the air in the shop warms, followed by that deep amber scent of his.

"Morning, lass."

"Morning," I answer as I continue to make my way around the counter. "What kind of coffee?"

"Same as yesterday. Pick a pastry, too."

I stop to look at him, trying to ignore the way my breathing halts every time I do. "You don't eat the pastries."

His eyes sparkle, the gold ring around his irises practically glowing in the morning light. "No, but I like knowing you've eaten something because I have a feeling you forgot to have breakfast."

Well, he really didn't need to call me out like that. "I don't forget," I answer slowly. "I just…get busy with other things."

"Uh-huh. Too busy if you ask me."

I lift my chin in defiance. "Good thing I didn't ask."

He raises an eyebrow, and I gulp, suddenly unsure about being so sassy. Grady's been nothing but kind to me, but he's still a bit…scary.

"I'll bring your pastry," I say hurriedly with a sweeter-than-usual smile as I slide his coffee to him.

To my relief, he nods and goes to his usual seat.

"Did you go to bed at a reasonable hour last night?"

The plate clatters to the table. Heat rushes right down to my core. Why am I turned on? And why does part of me want to say no just to see how he responds? The good girl side of me wants to make him proud even more, though.

"Yes. I went to sleep around eight-thirty. It was weird. I'm usually up until after midnight."

5

GRADY

That's going to change. Once she's with me, she'll have a strict bedtime. She'll also have breakfast every morning and not work at the ass-crack of dawn each fucking day.

I was pleased when I watched her leave her parents' house at eight last night. Much better than eleven like the night before.

"You need more sleep, Little one."

She huffs out a quiet laugh. "Okay, well, when I can actually find some time on my schedule, I'll make that happen."

Another thing that's going to change. Her schedule. From what I can tell, she goes non-stop all day. It's clear she isn't taking care of herself. The dark marks under her eyes give away her exhaustion. I don't know what is going on in her life. I've been forcing myself not to ask Chloe a bunch of questions because I want to get to know my girl on my own. It's getting harder and harder to resist, though. Especially since I only gain a tiny bit more information about her each morning I'm here.

"Why are you up so early?" she asks, eyeing me with a raised brow.

I shrug. "I'm an early riser."

What I'm not going to tell her is that I don't usually go to bed until past midnight most nights as well, and I'm lucky if I sleep a few hours. I'm the Daddy, though, and I can handle less sleep. She cannot.

A customer interrupts us, and, like every morning, I want to murder them for taking her attention away from me. I'm left watching her for an hour or so until my phone starts going off with calls and messages that need to be taken care of.

I pull out a new card from my jacket and scribble another note.

Eat. Bed by nine. Drink your water. And be good.

Then I drop a hundred on top of it and hide it with the plate.

When Friday morning rolls around, a sense of relief washes over me as I follow Katie to Twisted Bean. She doesn't know I'm trailing her, of course. I park across the lot and wait until she opens the shop to show my presence. I don't like that she drives to work by herself so early. Or that she drives home late in the evening from her parents' house. Although she headed home around eight again last night. Whether she's doing that because of the notes I've left her, I'm not sure, but it pleases me.

As soon as the open sign flickers on, I get out of my SUV and go inside.

"Morning, Little one."

She turns, and her eyes light up. She's happy to see me. The feeling is so fucking mutual. I count down the hours each night until I can get up and get dressed to come see her.

"Morning. Do you sit out there and wait until I open or something?"

Caught red-handed. "Aye. Need my morning fix."

"Of…coffee?" she asks slowly.

I shrug and lean against the counter as she starts making my drink.

"If I didn't know any better, I'd think you were stalking me," she says with a smirk.

She says it like it's a bad thing. It's not as if I'm some creep. I'm her future man. Her Daddy.

Instead of answering, I change the subject. "How was your night?"

Her gaze flicks to me, then back to the shots of espresso she's pouring. "Good. You?"

"Do anything fun?"

She slides the drink to me.

"I wouldn't really call cock fun." Her eyes bulge. "Oh my God, I just said cock. I meant caulk. Cau-aalk," she enunciates. "The white stuff that comes out of the long tube." Her cheeks turn bright red, and she ducks her head, trying to hide behind her hands. "Holy espresso beans."

I laugh, letting it roll up from my stomach. Jesus, she's so cute when she's embarrassed.

"It's okay, Little one. I'm glad it was caulk you were playing with and not the other thing. That would have seriously displeased me."

She peers at me between her fingers and sighs. "Can we start over? Good morning, Grady."

I wink at her. "Morning, lass. I'll just head to my table while you pick a pastry."

When I turn around, she blows out a deep breath, and I chuckle but don't say anything else.

The morning passes as usual, and when I leave, I scribble another note to leave with a hundred-dollar bill.

Eat. Bed by nine. Drink your water. Be a good girl. Looking forward to seeing you tonight.

"What do I need to know about her?" I lean back against my chair and wait for Chloe's answer. I want to know everything. Katie's favorite color. Favorite food. Favorite movie. What scares her. Is she into being dominated? Does she know anything about the lifestyle we all live? Any and every detail, no matter how minor, I want it. I'm tired of waiting to learn things little by little.

"Who?" Chloe asks as she sets plates and silverware on Declan's enormous dining table.

Bash barks out a laugh, and she grins so wide it's gotta be painful. She knows exactly who. She's being a brat on purpose. A spankable offense, if you ask me. Instead, her husband is practically cheering her on. He's so damn obsessed with Chloe that she could pretty much do anything, and he'd give her a high-five.

"Little girl, don't fuck with me. You know exactly who." I cross my arms over my chest and scowl at her. It only makes her smile even more.

"It's bad to curse in front of us. We're impressionable, you know. And we're not allowed to cuss, so you shouldn't either," she says, putting her hands on her hips and giving me a mock scowl.

"Jesus Christ," I mutter. "Chloe, I just need a little

help. What's something she likes? What would make her relax a bit around me?"

I'm practically to the point of pleading, but Katie's going to be here in a few hours. Even though I've seen her for five days straight, I still hardly know anything about her. I've never reacted to a woman this way. Never felt this connection that's drawing me to her like a magnet. She's meant to be mine. I feel it down to my bones.

Chloe sighs and plops down in a chair next to me. "She loves to read. She's a bit of an introvert, so reading is how she decompresses when she wants to unwind. Um, let me think... Oh, I know. Chocolate. She loves really good chocolate. Her dad used to ship in a special kind from Belgium every year for her birthday."

"She was close to her dad?" I ask.

Her face falls, and she bites her lip before she drops her shoulders. "Yeah. Her parents are both gone. They passed away several years apart from different illnesses."

A tightness settles in my chest to the point of pain. Making a fist, I rub the spot between my ribs. I did know about her parents passing. I was able to find that information easily on the internet.

"So she's all alone?"

Her bottom lip trembles as she nods. "I think so. Gosh, I feel so bad. I stayed in touch with her after I quit Twisted Bean, but I should have done more. She doesn't have any brothers or sisters, and I don't think she has time for many friends. Shit. I'm a horrible person."

Bash goes from amused to protective in a flash, pulling her up into his arms.

I rise, too, and reach out to stroke Chloe's hair. Bash glares at me, but I ignore him. The bastard is so fucking territorial with her, it's sickening.

"You're not a horrible person," I reassure her. "Life gets busy, and it's not like you did anything intentionally. Besides, you're trying to be her friend now."

Chloe slides her arms around Bash's waist and nods. "She's always been so sweet. I never met her dad, but her mom was wonderful when she was well. Katie never complained once about having to pick up extra shifts when her mom was sick or about taking care of her as her health declined."

In other words, Katie isn't used to being put first by herself or anyone else. Shame. She deserves to be spoiled rotten.

"Thanks for the info, Little one. Make sure I sit by her at dinner. And set Ronan on the other end of the table." I ruffle her hair and glance at Bash. He's smirking.

"Something funny, asshole?" I ask.

"More entertaining than anything. Watching you

lose your shit over a woman is so fucking amusing," Bash replies.

I knew I'd regret all the crap I gave him and the other guys when they first met their women. They were all so bent out of shape over their girls, and now I'm starting to see why. I already don't like the apartment complex Katie lives in. Once I get security cameras installed all over the property, I might feel a little better, but I'm going to hold off on those until I at least take her out on a date. Declan went full stalker on Cali. I'm trying not to follow in his footsteps. Even if I am following her to work every morning and home every night.

Six o'clock can't get here soon enough. I need to see her. Thanks to Bash, I've been peeking in on her all day. Apparently, when he was pining after Chloe, he tapped into the cameras at her work to keep an eye on her. The guy might talk a lot of shit, but he still has my back. We always have each other's backs. We're family, as fucked up as it may be.

While the girls are doing who knows what to get ready for the evening, I find my way into one of the smaller sitting rooms in the mansion. It's quiet and peaceful here. As soon as I sit on the plush couch, my eyes close, and my mind goes to Katie.

I want to pull her into my arms and hold her until she knows how fucking precious she is. She needs to be protected, coddled, spoiled, and taken care of. After watching her on the cameras, it's obvious she doesn't look after herself. I didn't see her eat once today, other than the pastry I left for her, nor did she take any breaks besides than a quick trip to the bathroom once in a while. She's going to wear herself into the ground unless something changes. And things will be changing because I *will* be her Daddy.

"Why is he in here?" Cali asks quietly.

Her voice startles me, but I don't open my eyes. I finally fell asleep.

"I don't know. Why is he asleep? Is he drunk? Maybe we should splash cold water on his face to see if he's still alive," Chloe answers.

"You even think about doing that, and you'll both go over my knee to get your bottoms spanked," I say evenly.

I finally open my eyes and turn to look at them. Cali, Chloe, Scarlet, and Paisley are in the doorway, grinning. Right next to them, Katie stands with her mouth hanging open. Her gaze is curious, though. My cock twitches. Is my girl wondering what it would be like to be put over my knee?

Then Chloe opens her sassy mouth again. "My Daddy won't let you spank me. He's too possessive for that. Nice try, butthead."

Katie's eyes widen as she gapes at Chloe. Does Katie have no idea what kind of lifestyle the girls live? Chloe would have told her before inviting her here, right?

Quickly, I rise and stride over to the women, my gaze glued to Katie. She watches me as I get closer, but she doesn't shrink back.

"Glad to see you made it," I say softly, lowering my head so it's slightly closer to hers. She has to tilt her chin up to look at me, and it takes herculean strength not to run my thumb over her plump bottom lip.

She lets out a soft exhale, smiles, then holds up a finger. "Just for the record, I wouldn't have splashed you with cold water."

The corners of my mouth twitch, and I wink at her. "Good thing, because you'd find yourself over my knee too if you did."

Her gasp is so loud that the other girls start laughing. Her pupils dilate, and her chest rises sharply.

"Grady is full of it," Scarlet tells her. "He's the softie of the family."

My skin heats as Katie runs her gaze from my face to my crotch and back up again. The girls might think I'm soft, but my cock hasn't been since the moment I met this woman.

"These girls are delusional if they think I wouldn't actually spank them if they deserved it," I say, staring at Katie. "You might not want to underestimate me."

She nibbles on her bottom lip, seeming to consider my threat.

"Dinner time," Declan calls out as he approaches.

All the women follow him toward the dining room with Katie at the rear. I trail behind. The entire way, her soft floral perfume has my cock at full attention. Thank goodness we'll be sitting at a table. Every so often, she looks over her shoulder at me and smiles shyly. I reach out and give one of her soft curls a playful tug.

I can't remember the last time I flirted with a woman, but fuck, this is fun. It's also a huge tease to my dick.

Chloe has placed name cards at each seat. Though she might be a bit of a brat, she put me and Katie next to each other like I asked, with Ronan at the other end. I catch her eye from across the room and wink. Chloe's lips curl into a smile, and she uses her fingers to make a heart sign in front of her chest. I guess she's forgiven for waking me up a few minutes ago.

Without missing a beat, I reach for Katie's chair

and pull it out for her, then push it in after she sits down, catching a whiff of her fruity shampoo.

"Would you like wine or something else to drink?" I ask quietly.

She looks over her shoulder and eyes me up and down again. "Wine, please."

As I pour her a glass, I can't stop glancing at her. She's beautiful. The permanent blush on her cheeks makes her look innocent. I find it hard to believe she doesn't have a man in her life. Chloe didn't think she was involved with anyone, and I sure as fuck hope that's the case because otherwise the guy will die.

All the food is set out family style. The guys like being able to make their girls' plates for them. One of the ways they show they care.

"Is there anything you don't want?" I ask as I pick up Katie's dinner plate.

She scans all the food, then looks to me and shakes her head. "No. It all looks delicious. You don't have to do that for me."

"Sit and relax, Little one. Drink your wine."

I reach for some tongs. Out of the corner of my eye, I see she takes a sip from her glass. My cock thickens. She's obedient. A pleaser. Just what I like. I have no way of knowing for sure, but I have a feeling she obeyed all the instructions I left for her this past week.

The girls spend the meal talking about so many different topics I can't keep up. I don't even try because the only one I want to pay attention to is the woman next to me.

She seemed shocked when I threatened to spank the girls. Does she know anything about this lifestyle? Or what a Daddy is? I'm not opposed to being with someone who's new to this kind of dynamic, but being a Daddy is something I can't turn off, so I really need her to be into it.

Maybe it's because I'm so controlling. That I feel the need to protect everyone around me. It could also be because I want to feel needed. It's probably fucked up that I want someone to be dependent on me, but I've never claimed to be normal. And what I want from Katie will be far from fucking normal. I'll want everything from her. Her submission, loyalty, obedience, attention. Every single thing.

"You're not eating." She has her big blue eyes turned up at me when I look over at her.

I glance at her plate and then back at her. "Neither are you."

A whisper of a smile spreads on her lips. "Yes, I am."

Cocking my head, I raise an eyebrow and pin her with a stern look. "You've been pushing your food around your plate all night. Start eating before I take it upon myself to feed you."

She scans the room to see if anyone is paying attention to our conversation.

"Are you always so concerned about people eating?" she asks.

No. Never. I'm not going to admit that, though. "Maybe. Depends on who it is, I guess. What do you do when you're not working?"

"Hmm. I don't really know." The sparkle in her eyes dims, and her shoulders drop. "That sounds like I don't have a life. I guess I don't. My mom passed away a few months ago, but she'd been sick for a while, so I usually spent all my time with her."

I lift my glass to my lips and take a drink, my heart squeezing for her. Fuck. This was not the direction I wanted the conversation to go.

"I'm sorry about your mom. She was lucky to have you."

We stare at each other for several seconds while everyone else around us talks.

"Right, Katie?" Chloe asks.

Katie's head snaps toward her friend. "Huh? I'm sorry, what did you say?"

Chloe grins. "I was telling Bash that we were planning a girls' night. Maybe we can go to a club or something."

"No clubs," Kieran says firmly.

"Maybe for you," Paisley argues, rolling her eyes at her husband.

Kieran grumbles something under his breath about

spanking her ass when they get home. Paisley winks at Katie.

Cali claps her hands. "We should go tonight!"

Paisley, Chloe, and Scarlet all shout their agreement while Katie bobs her head and grins.

Ronan returns from the kitchen with a new bottle of wine in hand. "None of you girls are going anywhere tonight. It's snowing."

"What?" Katie jumps up and runs from the room toward a window. "Oh, shoot!"

I follow her. Sure enough, big, fat white flakes are floating down from the dark sky.

"What's wrong?" Chloe asks.

Katie rushes toward the foyer. "I need to go. I can't drive in the snow. My tires are bald. I need to go before it gets worse."

Before she can reach the door, I step in front of her, stopping her in her tracks. "You're not going anywhere. It's really coming down out there, and it's below freezing. The hills around here are too steep, especially with bad tires."

My skin prickles. Why the fuck is she driving around in something so unsafe? She needs to be in a Range Rover or, better yet, an armored SUV of some kind.

"I… How will I get home?" she asks, her brows furrowed in confusion.

"You can stay the night here. I'm sure the girls have stuff you can wear."

"Ohh, slumber party! Daddy, can we have a slumber party? All of us?" Cali asks, her voice carrying through the whole house.

Chloe and Paisley bounce on their tiptoes and give Bash and Kieran pleading looks that have both men crumbling at their feet. And hell, I would be too if Katie looked at me like that.

"A slumber party?" she asks as though the idea is totally foreign to her.

"Yeah. A sleepover. The other girls do it all the time and end up sleeping on the couches in the theater room," I answer as I reach for her wrist.

Gently, I nudge her back toward the dining room, doing my best to ignore the lightning bolt between us. Fuck. Has anyone ever made me feel like this? "Let's finish eating."

"Tom said it was going to snow," she murmurs. "I didn't believe him because it's almost spring."

My entire body tenses, anger searing me from the inside out. "Who is Tom?"

He's a dead man. That's who.

6

KATIE

The edge in Grady's voice sends a zing of arousal through me. Is that jealousy? Possessiveness? Or am I imagining it?

"He's my friend. He's, uh... he's a homeless man who's been coming into the coffee shop since before my dad died. My parents were friends with him, too."

The muscle in his jaw tenses as he studies me. Chloe watches us intently, a grin on her face. Okay, I must have really been hearing what I thought I was. Why would Grady feel jealousy over little ol' me? I'm no one. Especially compared to him. Just a chubby girl with a coffee shop.

I have no idea what these guys do. When dinner is over, and I can get Chloe alone, I have a bunch of questions for her. Like, why do the girls all keep calling their men Daddy? Why did Grady threaten to spank her? Why are all these men in black suits like they're in the freaking mafia or something? Whatever they do, they're successful as hell because this mansion is probably about as big as the Pike Place Market.

"A homeless man? How did you meet him?" Grady asks.

Five more men turn their attention to me, their eyebrows pinched as they wait for an answer. Goodness, they're all so good-looking. How do Chloe and the other girls stand being around so much hotness all the time? I need a fan or something to cool me down.

"My parents met him a long time ago. He's a good man. I give him coffee most nights before I close the shop," I say softly. "Anyway, he always seems to know what the weather is going to do. He told me it was going to snow, but I didn't believe him because it's nearly spring. Guess I should trust his weather forecasting next time."

Especially since I'm panicking inside that I don't have Pancake with me. I've never gone a night without her. I might be a twenty-three-year-old woman with my own business, but I still need my stuffed bunny to be able to sleep. I'll sneak out after everyone goes to bed. Surely, it will stop snowing by then.

When we finish eating the best meal I've had in a long time, Grady picks up my plate and takes it—along with his—out of the room. I peek over at Chloe. She's practically glowing as she stares at me.

"Isn't he sweet? He's single, too," she whispers.

If my cheeks could actually catch fire, they would. I don't know why she informed me of his relationship status, but knowing he doesn't have a girlfriend pleases me beyond words.

"We should watch *Beauty and the Beast!*" Cali announces.

All the men groan, but Cali just rolls her eyes.

Scarlet giggles. "We watch it all the time. They love the movie, but they like to act like a bunch of curmudgeons. Do you like *Beauty and the Beast?*"

Grady's gaze is on me. I feel it as if he were actually touching me. Forcing myself to keep my eyes on Scarlet, I nod. "I love it. I want Beast's library."

Cali grins. "You should see Grady's library. It's huge. He has several first editions of really famous books."

I cock my head, surprised by that. Most people don't have a room for books in their houses unless they love to read. Grady doesn't give me bookworm vibes.

"You have a library?" I ask with a small smile.

"Aye. But if you tell me you read mob books like the rest of these girls do, I'm afraid I won't have a selection you'd like."

"Well, that's the thing about libraries," I reply. "They can always be added to. Everyone needs mob books in their collection."

Cali bursts out laughing while Grady looks at me like he isn't sure whether to laugh or roll his eyes.

"Jesus Christ. What is it with you girls and reading about men in the mafia? Declan asks.

"Like I keep telling you, Daddy. Someone's gotta show you guys how to run the mafia correctly. How are we supposed to know unless we read about it?" Cali shrugs.

My eyes practically bulge from my face. Did I just hear that right? How much wine did I drink?

"I take it from the look on your friend's face that she doesn't know what we do?" Bash asks.

Chloe comes around the table and grabs me by the hand. "Maybe we should go get the movie ready." Then she pulls me from the room with Cali, Scarlet, and Paisley following.

We're all silent as we walk through the house, the tension so thick I'm surprised we can't see it. I'm practically bursting with questions while panicking at the same time.

I'm momentarily distracted when we walk into an enormous room full of plush couches and a huge screen on the wall. There are blankets and pillows on every piece of furniture, and there's even a popcorn machine off to one side. Next to it, a display rack holds boxes of all different types of candy. The room is awesome. A movie-lover's dream for sure.

Once my amazement wears off, I turn toward the women. They all look a bit nervous.

"I have so many questions," I hiss quietly.

Chloe bobs her head. "I know. I'm sorry. I should have prepared you."

"Ya' think?" I ask. "Are they really in the mafia? And why do you all call them Daddy? And why did Grady threaten to spank you? Oh my God, I feel like I'm in a book right now or something. I mean, a snowstorm in March? Come on. This is just some wild dream I'm having. Right?"

I wait for one of them to confirm my dream theory, but none of them do. Instead, Chloe guides me to a couch and sits down with me.

"To answer your questions, yes. They're in the mafia," she says. "Actually, they kind of *are* the mafia. They're the top six of the Irish American Mafia. Declan is the boss."

My mouth drops open.

Chloe continues. "All of us call our men Daddy because they are Daddy Doms, and we're their submissives."

"They like to *think* we're their submissives. We're the ones who are actually in control," Paisley says with a smirk.

Scarlet snorts. "That's kind of true. I mean, they do discipline us if we disobey a rule or do something dangerous, but they also treat us like queens and pretty much give us anything and everything we want."

"It's not always sunshine and rainbows, though. They're difficult men. Controlling, possessive, jealous as hell. Most of the time, they're unreasonable and so freaking stubborn." Cali rolls her eyes. "But they love us unconditionally, and they would die for us."

I swallow, trying to absorb what they're telling me. I've read about Daddy Doms before. Several times, actually. I've even wondered if I'm a Little because of some of my mannerisms and the fact that I still sleep with a stuffed toy.

"Are you Littles?"

They look at each other like they're not sure how to answer. Chloe finally shrugs. "Sometimes? There are different degrees of being Little. None of us go super young, but we enjoy doing Little stuff like coloring, crafts, and watching Disney movies. Our Daddies like to treat us like we're Little a lot. They cut up our food and feed us sometimes, or they make us take naps or have an early bedtime. Basically, we don't really define what we are. We do what makes us happy and comfortable."

Huh. That sounds... pretty freaking amazing.

"Wait. Does that mean..."

"That Grady is a Daddy?" Scarlet asks. "Most definitely. I think he might be a bit surprising, though. He seems so easygoing, but I don't think he actually is.

He's super protective of all of us. It's interesting to see when he goes all Daddy-mode."

Before I have time to fully digest that and ask more questions, Grady and the rest of the men file in, all with drinks in their hands. A glass of wine in one and a glass of what looks like whiskey in the other. Except Ronan. He only has whiskey.

"Ready to watch the movie for the millionth time?" Killian asks.

Scarlet beams up at him. "So ready! I wonder if Beast is going to be nicer to Belle this time."

Killian snorts and rolls his eyes but then leans over to press a kiss to Scarlet's lips. "Let's hope, huh?"

She nods and cuddles up to his side when he sits down.

The couch I'm on is enormous, big enough for at least eight people. Chloe stays next to me, with Bash on her other side. Grady sits near but not too close. I'm not sure if I'm happy or disappointed. I smell his cologne, but I want more of it.

"Wine?" he asks, holding the stemmed glass out for me.

I take it from him and offer a smile. "Thank you."

The movie starts, the surround sound so good it feels like we're in the snow with Belle's father.

One of Grady's rings clinks against his glass as he takes a long drink, then looks at me. "The girls fill you in about us?"

A shudder runs through me. Does he mean about being in the mob? Or being Daddies?

"Yes," I whisper.

He stays quiet for a moment and takes another drink. "We might be bad men, Katie, but I need you to know you're completely safe with us."

Slowly, I turn my head to meet his gaze in the dim light. We stare at each other in silence, but it feels like we're communicating; I'm just not sure about what. I believe I'm safe with him. I believe Chloe and the other girls wouldn't be here if they didn't feel completely safe.

"I know."

As soon as I say it, his shoulders relax, and the tightness of his jaw releases. "Good girl."

The words are quiet, but in my head, they couldn't be any louder.

Good girl. Wow.

Who knew two words could be so beautiful? Could make me feel something I've never experienced before. Could make me want something I've only ever fantasized about.

When did my bed get so comfy?

I curl up tighter and feel around for Pancake. I

rarely let her go in my sleep, so panic creeps in as I search for her. My eyes fly open, and I look around the room. Crumb cake. This isn't my room. This isn't even my apartment. I must have fallen asleep during the movie.

Chloe is fast asleep at the other end of the couch, and Paisley is sprawled out on the thick carpet a few feet away. Scarlet is sleeping practically on top of her husband. He's snoring softly with his arm wrapped around her protectively. It's a pretty cute scene.

As quietly as possible, I peel back the fluffy blanket someone put over me and tiptoe from the room. I try not to think about the fact that it was most likely Grady who covered me up. At least, that's what I keep telling myself. It could have been any of the guys. I'm going with Grady, though.

I quietly make my way through the maze of a house toward the foyer. Hopefully, the snow will have melted so I can go home and snuggle up with Pancake. Otherwise, I'm not going to be able to sleep tonight. I can't believe I dozed off during the movie. I never do that.

"Where do you think you're going, Little one?"

I stop mid-step on the marble floor and slowly turn to find Grady. He's shed his suit jacket, tie, and shoes, but he still looks just as intimidating. His hair is a bit mussed like he's been running his fingers through it. The man looks so freaking edible, it's unfair.

"Oh, um, hi. I didn't mean to wake you," I whisper, even though we're alone in the enormous foyer.

His gaze is locked on me as he approaches, an eyebrow raised. "You didn't wake me. Where do you think you're going?"

His tone is even and quiet, but I feel the steel in it all the way down to my bones. How is that possible?

"I was going to check to see if it had stopped snowing so I can head home." I motion toward the large glass doors.

He narrows his eyes, and my clit tingles. I don't think he likes my answer.

"It has stopped snowing, but you're not driving home in the middle of the night with the streets still wet and slick."

Squaring my shoulders, I stand a bit taller. Which isn't much compared to him. The man towers over me. It's both hot and unnerving. "You can't tell me what I can and can't do."

Whoa. Where did that come from? I'm not normally the sassy type. Especially to authoritative figures, and Grady definitely falls into that category.

The gold in his irises flickers. "Can't I? Because I have your keys in my pocket, so I'm pretty sure I can."

I glare at him and put my hands on my hips. "How did you get my keys?"

"They were sitting right on top in your purse."

"You went through my purse?" I shriek, still somewhat quietly.

His lips curl up into an ominous grin. "No. I opened your purse, and they were right there. I didn't look through anything. Would I have found something naughty in there if I had?"

Heat creeps over my cheeks, and I scoff. "No."

At least I hope he wouldn't find anything. He'd really have to search for the secret zipper inside. Every purse needs a secret vibrator compartment if you ask me. It's probably not actually meant for hiding toys, but it's freaking brilliant.

"Uh-huh," he says. "You need to go back to sleep."

My prickly demeanor disappears, and I drop my hands to my sides. "I can't sleep here. I don't know how I fell asleep in the first place."

His expression softens. "Easy. With your feet in my lap and your head on the pillow. Why can't you sleep here?"

Oh God. How embarrassing. "I put my feet in your lap?"

"Yes. I like the pastel pink polish you have on. You didn't answer my question. Why can't you sleep here?"

He looked at my toes? It'd be nice if a hole would open for me to drop into right about now. Thank goodness I painted my toenails last night. He shouldn't have sat by me if he didn't want my feet on him. Although, he doesn't seem to mind.

"Um, I just don't sleep well if I'm not in my bed. What time is it?" I scratch my temple and look around for a clock.

"Three. Why don't you sleep well if you're not in your bed?" he shoots back.

Tilting my head to look up at him, I smirk. "Are we playing twenty questions?"

His mouth curves into a cocky smile. "Do you want to play twenty questions?"

"Not at three in the morning. Why are you still awake?" I ask.

He shrugs. "I don't sleep much."

Huh. That's too bad. I love sleeping. Especially when I have Pancake. "Why not?"

"Now who's playing twenty questions?"

I roll my eyes and sigh. This man is exasperating. Does he have this much stamina in other parts of his life? Oh, God, what the hell is wrong with me? "I'll be fine to drive home."

"You're not driving home. It's out of the question," he says firmly. His tone leaves no room for argument. Too bad, arguing with him is kind of fun.

"It's not your decision to make. I'm an adult, you know?"

Leaning down until his face is only a few inches from mine, he looks me directly in the eye. "Are you? Because you might be of legal age, but when I look at you, I see a sweet innocent girl who needs someone to take care of her."

I tremble. My nipples ache. My core clenches. His words are intimate. Special. And so damn true, it's terrifying.

"I'm an adult," I reply breathily.

He tilts his head to the side, keeping his gaze on me. "Uh-huh. You're still not driving home."

With a huff, I cross my arms over my chest. "Fine. I'll order a car service."

"Nope. Not happening. If you try to get into a stranger's car, the consequences will be dire."

My mouth falls open as I stare up at him. "You can't threaten to spank me!"

I take a small step back, suddenly nervous. I've never been spanked before.

Grady takes a step toward me, clearly enjoying this game of intimidation. "I didn't threaten to spank you."

"You implied it, like you did with the other girls."

He shrugs and then shakes his head. "No, I didn't. I was referring to the driver of the car service. Inviting a stranger onto mafia property with a bunch of overprotective gangsters? Do you think that's a wise choice, baby? Do you want their blood on your hands?"

What. The. Fuck? He wouldn't do that. Right? Shit. I'm so out of my depth here. I need to get Chloe alone and ask her more questions. Like, do they actually torture and kill people? Or is it nothing like it is in the books? Yeah, unlikely. I may not know Grady well, but all it takes is one look to know he's done some bad stuff. He's dangerous and deadly, and it would be smart not to push him.

"I didn't think so. If you want to go home so badly, I'll drive you, though I'd prefer you to stay here," he adds.

The look on my face must be enough of an answer because he sighs. "Okay, Little one. Go get your shoes on, and I'll take you home."

My shoulders relax, and I shoot him a soft, grateful smile before I head back to the theater room for my stuff. With each step I take, the wetness between my legs grows. I try to ignore it so I don't have to think about what it means. Like why I love how he just dominated the hell out of me and called me baby. Yep, definitely ignoring that.

7

GRADY

A disgruntled feeling settles over me as I drive her home. I don't want to take her there. Why is it so important for her to go to her place anyway? The estate is much more comfortable.

"I'll come pick up my car in the daylight."

Slowly, I turn to look at her, my eyebrows raised. "And how do you plan to get up here, Little one? Because I think we already talked about you taking a car service."

I've always been protective of the girls in our family, but with Katie, it's like it goes into overdrive. I want to wrap her in a bubble. *My* bubble. That way, I can keep her safe forever.

"I can have a friend bring me," she answers cautiously.

The muscles at the back of my neck tense. A

friend. Let her show up with a male friend. He'll disappear so fucking quickly. The only reason her friend Tom isn't already on my hit list is because I'm assuming he's much older if her parents were friends with him.

"I'll bring your car to you. What time do you go to work?"

"I'm working noon to close today."

The streets are wet, but the temperature has come up, so it's not frozen. It's almost as if it never snowed. Typical for Seattle. We rarely get anything that sticks around. Cali is going to be so disappointed when she wakes up.

"I'll bring your car at eleven."

That will give me time to get a new set of tires for her and have a mechanic check it out. If I thought she wouldn't protest, I'd bring her a whole new car, but I don't think we're there yet. At least, she's not.

"Thank you, Grady. Sorry you're stuck doing all of this." She motions to me driving.

I reach out, and her eyes trail to my hand as I run the back of my index finger over her cheek. "I'm not stuck doing anything, princess. I do what I want."

Her pupils dilate as she lets out a breath, and I lower my arm. My cock is painfully hard. It has been all night around her.

"Tell me why you wanted to come home to sleep so badly." I'm tired of asking. There is a reason she didn't want to stay, and I want to know what it is. I want to know every single thing about her.

When she opens her mouth, I hold up my hand to stop her because she's about to lie to me.

"Just remember, lying is naughty, and naughty girls get in trouble."

Her mouth snaps shut as she stares at me in disbelief. She's silent for several seconds while I continue to drive through the dark streets.

"It's a silly reason."

"Nothing you say is silly."

She sighs and turns her head to look out the passenger window. "I have a stuffed rabbit I sleep with. My dad gave it to me when I was a kid. I can't sleep without it. I know that sounds childish—"

I grab her hand to stop her and stroke my thumb over it. "It's not childish. There's nothing wrong with sleeping with a toy. Cali and the rest of them do, too. What's its name?"

When she doesn't answer right away, I look over and find her staring at me as if I'm an alien. I squeeze her hand and quirk a half-smile at her.

"Pancake," she murmurs.

Chuckling, I nod. "Pancake is a cute name."

Even though a lot of adults have stuffed animals, the fact that she can't sleep without it confirms my suspicions. She has Little tendencies. I noticed it the first time I met her when she had a cute scrunchie at the base of her ponytail. Then again, when I showed up at the shop the next day, she put rainbow sprinkles on top of her coffee. And tonight, when I covered her up after she fell asleep, she pulled the fuzzy blanket up to her face and ran it over her cheek. She might be an adult, but she's going to be Daddy's Little girl one day very soon.

When we arrive at her apartment, I get out and round the car to open the door for her.

"Thank you," she says as she rocks back and forth on the balls of her feet.

"You're welcome. I'll walk you to the door."

She looks like she's about to argue but thinks better of it before she turns and leads the way to her apartment.

"How'd your rabbit get the name Pancake?" I don't know why I ask, but something tells me the name is important.

Katie stops and looks up at me, sadness shining in those pretty blue eyes. "Every Saturday morning, my dad would let my mom sleep in, and he would make pancakes for the two of us. He always made mine in the shape of a bunny. We'd sit on the couch and watch cartoons while we ate." A slow smile spreads on her lips. "Before he died, he told me to keep the Saturday tradition alive for as long as I could."

My throat tightens. Fuck. I wish I'd been able to

meet her father. He sounds like a good man. "How long did you keep it up?"

She beams at me. "I never stopped."

I stare at her for a long time before I can swallow. "One day, maybe you'll let me join you."

When she doesn't say anything right away, panic rises within me. Did I push it too far? We don't even know each other, and I'm already trying to intrude on a tradition she held with her late father. Real fucking sensitive of me.

Then she knocks me on my ass.

"Maybe. It depends how good you are at making a bunny pancake." She pushes the door open. "See you at eleven."

I SMELL the brown sugar before I reach her door. Cinnamon and nutmeg linger around it, too. Whatever she's making, I want some. I can work out extra hard in the gym to make up for some sweets. Especially if Katie made them.

As soon as she answers the door, my protective Daddy side kicks into high gear. Something's wrong.

She looks at me, her blue eyes a bit wild and confused. "Um, hi."

My gut twists as I step inside, nudging her back into the apartment. I look around, scanning for danger. Or anything that explains why Katie's clothes from last night are covered in flour, her hair is plopped on top of her head in a big messy bun, and she has dark marks under her eyes like she hasn't slept.

When I don't see anything to be concerned about, I take in her place. It's cozy. Small. But it screams Katie. Lots of pink and cream shades, all blending together perfectly. Fairy lights and lamps create a relaxing ambiance. This is definitely her safe space. Here and the coffee shop.

"What's wrong, baby?" I finally ask, furrowing my eyebrows.

She runs the back of her hand over her cheek and leaves a trail of flour on her skin. Unable to resist, I reach out and brush it away.

"What? Nothing's wrong. I'm fine. Why would anything be wrong?" she laughs nervously, then spins around and goes back to the small kitchen.

I guess we're going to have to make no lying a clear rule between us because my naughty girl just fibbed, and I don't like it. If something is bothering her, I want to know. I want her to tell me every single emotion she's feeling all the time. Because if she's sad or anything other than happy, I will fix it.

"Katie," I say in a hushed voice as I follow her.

"Everything's fine. Just great. I had dinner at a

mobster's house, and I'm pretty sure my friend is trying to hook me up with one of her mobster friends, and I've never even broken a single rule in my life, yet I'm pretty sure they kill people for fun, and then I go and blab about my dad and bunny pancakes, and that was something special between us, and I've never even had a boyfriend." She flings a spatula around as she speaks, sending batter everywhere. "And I don't even know if you like me, that's how inexperienced I am. I also don't know anything about being Little or having a Daddy, and they told me you're a Daddy, and I don't know what that means. And I have to sell my parents' house, and the realtor wants me to do a bunch of crazy things before putting it up for sale, and all I want to do is sell it and be done with it so I can move on and maybe start having a life, but I'm also afraid to move on because I can't remember the last time I didn't have someone or something to take care of, and I'm freaking out here."

Before she covers her entire kitchen in batter, I stride over to her and take the spatula. After I toss it in the sink, I grab a towel and turn back to her to take one of her hands in mine. She stares up at me, glassy-eyed and sad, and it breaks my fucking heart. I start cleaning her up while I keep my gaze on her.

"Princess, breathe. In and out." She does while we stare at each other. "Good girl. That's it. Good."

I keep wiping flour and batter from her skin. "First, let's get one thing straight. I am interested in you. I'm trying to move slow, and it's fucking torture. But I also know it's what you need, and you come first. Always. Just so we're clear, though, I'm only going to go at this pace for a limited time before I lose my patience and we start moving at my speed."

Her mouth drops open. It nearly kills me not to take advantage of that and start kissing her. It's not the right time, though. If she's been up panic baking all morning, she's not in any frame of mind for me to be kissing her. She needs me to take control and take care of her.

"Secondly," I say, using the towel to wipe her chin, "we don't kill people for fun. We don't kill people unless it's necessary. And you will never be around that. You will never be involved with that side of my life. For the most part, the mafia is just another business. I'm not going to sugarcoat it and tell you I'm a law-abiding citizen because I'm not. I have pools of blood on my hands, but it will never be your blood. You will continue being my rule-following girl because that's one of the reasons I like you. You're pure and sweet and a good girl. I need some good in my life, princess."

She bites her lip and stares at my chest. I think I'm getting through to her. I just admitted to killing people. It's possible she might decide to call the police on me here in a second.

"You don't have to be any certain type of Little. You just be you. As far as being a Daddy Dom, yes, I am. I thrive on control. I want to be the one in control of a relationship. I make the rules. I would expect you to follow them. Mostly because the rules are meant to keep you safe, healthy, and happy. I will take care of you, make sure you're eating, sleeping, not working too much, things like that. The kind of relationship I want isn't always easy. There will be times when you don't like my decisions or when you have to face the consequences of being naughty, but that's just how it is. I'm not easy, princess."

When I'm finally satisfied with my clean-up job, I toss the towel aside and hook my finger under her chin. "Lastly, I will never intrude on your Saturday morning tradition unless you want me to. I understand that's something special you had with your dad. I would never do anything to tarnish that. If you want to eat bunny pancakes and watch cartoons by yourself every Saturday, I'll find something to do elsewhere. Understand?"

Tears fill her eyes, wetting her long lashes. I tug her into me, wrapping my arms around her softness. When she slides her hands around my waist and hugs me back, the only thing that exists is her.

"I'm scared," she whispers.

"I know, baby. I got you, though."

"You don't even know me. Do you really want to

get involved with this?" she asks, stepping back and motioning to herself.

I look her up and down, a grin curving my lips. "Yeah, baby. I sure the fuck do. And if you question me again about wanting you, we'll talk about it with you over my knee."

Her mouth drops open, and I chuckle. Then she yawns, and all my laughter disappears.

"Have you been baking since I dropped you off?"

"Um, yes. I stress bake, and well, do you want a muffin? Or a strudel? I also made banana bread, a lemon loaf, two different kinds of cookies, and a coffee cake."

Jesus Christ.

She turns toward the counter. "I could pack some up to send home with you to share with Bash and the rest of the guys."

Grabbing the edge of the counter on either side of her, I pin her in place, her back to my front and lean down so my mouth is close to her ear. "If you ever try to share your sweets with my friends, you won't like the consequences, Little one."

Pleasure rips through me when she shudders and pushes back against me. "It's just food," she murmurs.

I nuzzle her neck, scraping my short beard against her skin. "I don't care. I don't share. *Ever*."

She sucks in a breath, and when she finally nods, I

take a step back. "Come on, princess. Time to get into bed."

"What? No, I can't. I have to go to work."

"No, you need to go to bed. You only slept for two hours at Declan's last night. You're not working on a couple hours of sleep."

She bites her lip and peers up at me. "I have to. One of my employees is out of town, and the other has class today. I can't ask my opener to stay until close."

Shit. I need to tread carefully. She's the owner of the shop, which means she's the boss. A good one at that.

Fucking lightbulb.

I pull out my phone and call Bash.

"Yeah?" he answers.

"What are you and Chloe doing today?"

"We don't have plans. She slept in and is just now having breakfast."

"Good. Can she do a shift at Twisted Bean? You can go with her and keep your stalker eye on her all day."

Katie shakes her head and tries to reach for my phone, but I step back.

"Grady, no," she hisses.

"Why? Was she a bad employee?"

Her eyes widen like I've slapped her. "What? No. She was a great employee. I can go to work. I'm fine. I'll rest tonight."

Bash chuckles in the background. "Daddying her already, huh? Nice, man, nice. Yeah, we can be there in an hour. Chloe's excited. She loved working there."

"There. That's taken care of. Bedtime," I say after I hang up.

Katie stares at me, unblinking. "Did you really just do that?"

"Yes. Come on, baby." I gently grab her shoulders and nudge her toward the only bedroom, checking to make sure the oven is off and there's nothing in it before I leave the kitchen.

"Is that… Is that how this is going to work? You do whatever you want and think I'm going to go along with it?" she asks.

Now she's catching on. The sooner she gets with the program, the better. She can fight it, but the end result will still be the same.

"Yes, baby." I look around her room, taking in everything I can. Just like the living room, it's done in soft pinks and creams. Her bed is made, and right on top of her pillow is an old, tattered bunny I assume is Pancake.

"Where are your pajamas?" I doubt she'll let me change her clothes for her, even though I'd prefer to be the one to do it. It's a Daddy's job, after all.

"Um, I'll get them," she answers as she fidgets with her hands. "I really am fine to work. I've gone in on less sleep than this before."

A growl escapes my throat as I glare at her. "And that will never happen again going forward. Are we clear? If you don't get a full eight hours of sleep, you don't go to work."

She stops and stares at me like I've lost my mind. Then she starts laughing and waving her hand in the air. "Oh my gosh. I just realized that Chloe's pranking me. This is all a prank. Oh, God, I can't believe I thought this was real."

Her laughter turns into a cackle, and I can't help but smile. My sweet Little girl is living in denial.

"It's not a prank, princess. This is all real. I'm real. Now, unless you want to find yourself over my lap before you go to sleep, I suggest you pick out some pajamas and get changed."

Almost immediately, she stops laughing. "You can't threaten to spank me all the time."

This time, I laugh as I cross the room to her and capture her chin between my fingers. Her pupils dilate, and she stops breathing for a second. My cock aches for her. It's torture taking my time. Especially when I want to bury myself deep inside her pussy and never leave it.

"I can threaten to spank you whenever I want, baby. Don't worry; some spankings you're going to love and want more of. Some of them will even end in screaming orgasms."

8
KATIE

His touch is so warm. Gentle, but firm. It's like anytime he holds me, I melt right into him.

When he threatens to spank me, my body heats, and my pussy clenches. Spanking scenes in books are always my favorite parts but I have no idea if I'd actually enjoy it. What if it's not as hot as it is in the stories? Grady made it clear that some spankings won't be pleasurable.

Could I submit to being punished? The idea is intriguing. Being forced to strip out of my pants and panties and bend over his thighs so he can discipline me like a naughty Little girl? Yeah, the thought is freaking hot. I have a feeling it might not feel as sexy, though, when it's actually happening.

"I, um, Grady?" I say softly.

I'm so tired and confused right now that I don't know what to think about all of this. This man I just met is bulldozing into my life, and I don't know how to react. I've never had a man show interest in me like this, and I'm pretty sure most men aren't quite this… intense.

"I know, baby. This is a lot. For now, I want you to shut your brain off and focus on getting ready to sleep. Find something to wear and get changed. I'm going to cover all your baked goods. I'll be back in five minutes. I want you under those blankets with Pancake in your arms when I get back. Can you be a good girl and do all that for me?"

His voice is soft, coddling, but he's not asking, and I know it. I also want to please him and be his good girl. "Yes."

When he leans down and presses a kiss to my forehead, I suck in a breath and close my eyes. I want him to kiss me everywhere. I want to feel the scratchiness of his beard on my skin, my nipples, lower. I've never felt this need before. It's overpowering all my senses.

As he takes a step back, my gaze lands on his slacks and the enormous bulge between his legs. Holy crap. That's big. Long and thick.

"Eyes up here, princess. Ignore that. I can't help my response to you."

I snap my head back, though the look on my face

must be one of shock because he chuckles softly as he turns around and leaves me alone to spiral.

A full minute passes before I start moving. Shoot, I need to hurry up before he gets back. I dig through my drawers and find the least ratty matching pajama set I have. One of these days, I'll go buy some new ones. It's been on my list of things to do forever, but life has gotten in the way. I can't remember the last time I bought any new clothes or shoes.

Right as I climb under the covers, Grady taps on the door, then walks in and gives me that breathtaking smile of his. Who knew teeth could be so white and perfectly straight? The man is a mix of sophistication and roughness. His teeth are perfect, but his nose is crooked as though it's been broken a time or two. He wears designer suits, but he's covered in tattoos. He looks like he'd be at home in a boardroom. He also looks like he could kill a man with his bare hands. He's a complete contradiction. A hot one.

"I don't know what you put in those blueberry muffins, but I ate three, and I'm taking the rest home," he says as he sucks on the tip of his index finger.

My breathing increases, and my nipples bud into points. Good God. Does he realize how sexy he is, or is he blind to what he does to women? When he winks at me and gives me a cocky grin, I giggle and shake my head. The man knows exactly what he's doing. Bastard.

He sits on the edge of my bed. "Who's your realtor?"

"Calvin Dunlap," I answer without thinking. "Why?"

There's a flutter low in my tummy as I study him. He's flawless, and here I am, looking like a hot mess express.

"Do you know the guy well?" His voice is tight. Controlled. Too controlled. Is he jealous? The thought shouldn't thrill me, but my pussy disagrees.

"No. I don't. He was recommended. I don't like him very much, but this is all new to me, so I'm just trying to get through it as quickly as possible to pay off my parents' final hospital bills before the bank tries to come after the business."

Suddenly, everything feels heavy. My body. My eyes. My heart. I'm tired. So tired. And it's not my lack of sleep that's causing it.

As though he senses it, he reaches out and brushes some wild hairs away from my face. "I want you to sleep. Will you be a good girl and do that, or do I need to sit here and make sure you rest?"

I have a feeling he isn't bluffing.

"I'll sleep. You need to go to work or something, I'm sure. Wait, do you actually go to work?"

I need to ask Chloe some questions. A whole lot of them because my head is spinning. The mafia? Seriously?

He lets his fingers dwell on the side of my face, his touch settling something inside me. Is it possible for someone to do bad things but still be a good person? I've always felt that I'm a good judge of character, and something tells me that Grady is a great man.

"Yes. I do. I have people who report to me. We all have roles. It's like one enormous business with Declan as the CEO. The other five of us are senior employees. Most of our fathers were in the top six."

Interesting. He almost makes it seem boring.

"Your father was in the mafia, too?"

Grady looks away, his jaw clenched, pain etched in his features. "Aye. He was." Then he stands and leans over me, placing his hands on either side of my head. "You need to rest. I'm leaving my card right here on your nightstand next to your phone. Text me when you wake up. Understand?"

I want to ask more questions. I've pretty much blabbed my entire life story, but I don't know anything about him. Now isn't the time, though.

"Yes."

"Good girl," he murmurs.

Then he bends down and presses a feather-light kiss to my forehead. "Sweet dreams, princess."

Katie: *Can we get together? I have a bazillion questions.*

Chloe: *LOL. I've been waiting to hear from you. Grady dropped off some muffins for me and told me you were napping. It was cute. He got all growly when Bash tried to eat one.*

The corners of my lips twitch. Jealousy isn't supposed to be hot, but there's something about Grady getting all possessive that's sexy as hell. He seems chill, but I have a feeling he's quite intense.

Katie: *He showed up when I was in the middle of panic baking.*

Chloe: *Ooh, girl. Panicking over him?*

Unable to wait for answers, I press the call button.

"Hey," she says.

"Yes, totally panicking over him," I blurt out. "This is a lot. He's a lot. I feel like a mouse being stalked by the cat."

"It's hot, right?"

"Chloe!" I squeal.

She bursts out laughing. "Listen, these guys are a bit unconventional. They don't live by a set of rules. They do what they want. When they find someone they want, they go after them. The second Bash got permission from my brother, he was all over me, completely unrelenting."

"You're supposed to be making me feel better."

"I'm trying. Just listen. I'm getting there. They're animals. Really good-looking animals. But they're also protective, and they treat us like we're royalty. Just give him a chance. You've spent the last fifteen years taking care of your parents. They were wonderful people, but because of their illnesses, you always came second. Maybe you should let Grady take care of you now."

That does sound wonderful. The way he showed up and took control when I wasn't able to think clearly? That was exactly what I needed. He took my choices away from me, but only for my own good.

"What about what they…do. For work," I say slowly, trying to figure out how to bring it up over the phone.

She sighs. "I'm not going to pretend it's not scary. They face risks. It's dangerous. But they're also smart."

I rub Pancake's ear between my fingers, my mind running in circles. "I don't know. I'll think about it."

"Uh-huh. I bet you will. You'll be thinking about that hot Irishman making you scream," she taunts, giggling.

Heat spreads over my cheeks as I grin. I'm sure with the outline in his pants I saw earlier, he could definitely make me scream.

"Thanks for working at the shop for me. I'll write you a check tomorrow."

Chloe snorts. "Love the change of subject, and no, you won't. I had fun. I wouldn't mind taking a shift once in a while."

My heart squeezes. "I'd like that."

"Oh, Tom stopped by. Bash almost blew a vein when I hugged him."

Laughing, I roll my eyes. These guys are over the top. And the fact that I like that about them is a bit frightening.

"Who are you talking to?" Grady asks in the background.

"Katie," Chloe answers.

My stomach tightens. Shoot. I haven't texted him yet. It only took a few minutes for me to fall asleep after he left, and I slept like a baby. Once I woke up, I needed to talk to Chloe.

There's a rustling sound. "I believe you were supposed to message me when you woke up, princess." His voice is deep and stern, but there's also a hint of care. "I was getting worried about you."

I suck in a breath. "You were?"

"Yes. Why didn't you text me?"

"Sorry. I needed to talk to Chloe first."

He sighs. "Still overthinking it, baby?"

Rubbing Pancake's thin ear again, I close my eyes and smile. It's like he knows me already. "Yes. A little."

"Was Chloe helpful?"

"Yes."

"Good. I'm coming over and bringing dinner. Be there in about half an hour."

I bolt up in bed. "Wait, but…"

He hung up on me. Seriously?

Remembering that he left his phone number, I grab the card from the nightstand.

"Yeah, princess? Did you need something else besides dinner?" he asks.

"What? No. I mean, you don't have to come over. I can find something here. I have work to do anyway, and I promised my neighbor I would bake her some cakes for her son's birthday, so I should work on that, too. Thanks for the offer."

The line is silent for a few seconds, so I look at my phone to make sure the call is still connected. Then he chuckles deeply, and my core tightens at the sound.

"That's not how this works, baby girl. I'll be over in thirty with dinner, and we'll go from there. We'll also be having a discussion about you overdoing things and not taking care of yourself first."

This time, when I open my mouth to argue, no words come out. I take care of myself. I mean, sure, I don't remember the last time I washed my hair. Or painted my nails. Or bought new clothes. But it's fine. I don't need any of that stuff. Even though I often wish I had the time and energy for it.

"See you soon, baby."

"Uh-huh," is my only reply because what else is there to say? Grady O'Brien doesn't ask permission. He does what he wants, and tonight, he wants to come over. And I still look like a walking disaster.

Shower. A shower would help. Maybe I can even

take a minute to shave. Yep. Shaving is a must. Not that anything is going to happen. Nope, it definitely won't.

9

GRADY

"You're being pushy." Chloe crosses her arms and glares at me as I slide my phone into my pocket.

"Yeah? Does that surprise you?"

She studies me for a beat, then drops her arms. "Not really. It's how you guys do things. It's annoying but also kind of hot."

"Excuse me?" Bash asks, turning his head to look at us from his seat on the couch. "Did you just call Grady hot? Do you want your ass reddened tonight? You're already in trouble for hugging that Tom guy."

Chloe looks at me and rolls her eyes. She's not the least bit worried about her husband's threats. He hands them out like candy on Halloween, but I have a feeling that when it comes down to it, she rarely gets disciplined.

"Who is this Tom guy? Katie brought him up last night. Do I need to worry about him?" I question Bash.

"Of course not," Chloe answers before Bash has the chance. "He's an old homeless man. Katie gives him free coffee and leftover pastries and offers to wash his clothes and blankets. He never lets her, though."

That sounds exactly like my girl. Always giving. Always offering her help even when her own cup is empty. And from what I've seen, it's past the point of empty. She's exhausted and has way too much on her shoulders. It's time for her to offload some of her load to me.

Ignoring Chloe, I look back at Bash and raise my eyebrows.

He shrugs and shakes his head. "I don't think you have to worry about him. He seems harmless, but if I were you, I'd check him out. Can never be too careful when it comes to our girls."

"I'll add him to my list. First is the realtor, who I have a bad feeling about. Does the name Calvin Dunlap ring any bells with you?" I ask. "Something about the guy isn't sitting right with me."

Bash thinks about it for a second. "No. But you know who's got information about anyone worth knowing in this city…"

"Yeah. Cage Black." I lift my shoulders. "You think he's still going to talk to us after Kieran punched him?"

"Who did I punch?" Kieran strides into the living room with Paisley by his side.

"Cage Black," Bash answers.

Kieran holds his hands up. "He asked for it."

That's kind of true. I'm pretty sure Cage goaded Kieran just to be an ass and knew he'd either get shot or punched.

I snort and shake my head when Kieran grabs his girl by the hips and moves her to the other side of him, farther away from me. Possessive bastard.

Paisley shoots him an exasperated glare and pinches his side. "You need therapy."

Kieran wraps his arm around her and presses a kiss to the top of her head. "I know, Little demon. You're my therapy, though."

A pang of jealousy swirls in my chest. I want that. I want what my friends have, and I want it with Katie.

"I'd like to stay here and watch you two idiots be all protective over your girls, but I'm gonna go take mine dinner."

Because she will be my girl. Soon.

THE DOOR SWINGS OPEN, and my heart races. Droplets of water stain Katie's soft lavender sweater from thick tendrils of wet hair hanging over her shoulders. Her unadorned cheeks flush pink. Black leggings hug her lush thighs. My cock goes rigid. Fuck, she's gorgeous.

"Hey, princess."

Her cheeks flush, and she dips her head as she steps back to let me in. I go straight to the kitchen and set down the bag of food, then stride back to her. She gasps as I yank her against me, wrapping her in a hug.

A few seconds pass before she slides her hands around my waist and hugs me back, relaxing into my embrace.

"You're in trouble, you know," I murmur against her hair.

Just as I expect, she pulls back and looks up at me in shock. "What? Why? I didn't do anything."

Using my thumb and index finger, I grab her chin and raise my eyebrows. "Really? What did I tell you to do when you woke up?"

Her entire body does a little shudder, and my cock grows harder. Does she like the idea of being in trouble?

"I was going to…" She trails off.

"But you didn't. You called Chloe instead. When your Daddy gives instructions, he expects to be obeyed."

As she stares up at me, her chest stutters, and her

pupils dilate. "I don't have a Daddy," she replies, barely above a whisper.

The corners of my lips curve into an evil smile. "Don't you, princess? Because I think you want a Daddy. I think you want me. Am I wrong?"

We're so close that our mouths are nearly touching, and I can practically taste the cherry-scented lip gloss she has on. I inch closer until my lips brush against hers. I'm trying to hold back. I want her more than I've ever wanted any woman in my life. The animal in me wants to ravage her, but the Daddy in me knows she isn't ready.

"Not completely wrong," she pants.

At least she gave me that. Knowing that she has similar feelings about me is enough of a nugget for me to hold onto until the next step.

"Let me be clear right now. If I give you a command or rule, I expect you to follow it. If I cross one of your limits, you say red, and I stop immediately. Understand?"

She studies me for a few seconds. "It's a bit soon for a safeword, isn't it? We're only friends."

I chuckle. "Chloe and the rest of the girls can use their safewords with any of us at any time and we'll immediately stop what we're doing and figure out what's wrong. So, no, it's never too soon for a safeword, princess."

Her light blue eyes darken, my words lingering

between us. Finally, she nods. "Okay. But I'm not yours to punish. And you can't come over here whenever you want. I could have had plans."

I clench my jaw, squeezing her hips even tighter. "Did you have plans, princess? Because if you did, call him right over here, and I'll make sure he knows you two will never have plans again."

She gasps, her mouth hanging open. "Grady! That's not what I meant. I'm not seeing…or dating…or whatever with anyone."

Thank fuck. I was already pretty sure that was the case, but hearing it from her mouth settles the persistent doubt that's been hovering.

"That's good, baby. And you won't be seeing or dating or doing whatever with any other man ever again. The only man you'll do those things with is going to be me."

I'm being pushy, but I can't help it. I need her commitment. I need to know that she's not going to talk to, call, text, entertain, smile at, fuck, or fall for any other man. That she's as committed to me as I'm ready to be with her.

"Grady, I don't understand." She blinks several times, her face twisted with confusion. "We've only known each other for a week. We come from two different worlds, and you could surely do better than someone like me."

Rage rips through me, and I tighten my hands until

she lets out a whimper from the bruising touch on her hips. "If I ever hear you say something to put yourself down like that again, you'll be in trouble."

What I really want to tell her is that I'll bare her ass and put her over my knee to paddle her until she's a sobbing mess and understands that putting herself down is against her rules.

"I'm not putting myself down, Grady. It's fact. I'm basically poor and you're rich. We're from two different worlds, and they don't tend to mix well."

"Is that so, princess? You think you and I wouldn't mix well? I think we'd be perfect together. I'd protect and take care of you, and you'd be the softness I need after a long day. You'd be my everything. You wouldn't be poor because my money would become yours. Fuck society. I dress in a suit, but I'm a criminal. You're classy and way too good for someone like me, but you think that's going to stop me? Sure the fuck not."

We're so close that the soft swell of her tummy presses against my cock. She can feel it, and from the glassy look in her eye, I'd say she likes it.

"You're crazy. I don't know why you want me," she murmurs, her shoulders hunched slightly.

I push her against the counter, blocking her in. Taking a fistful of her hair, I carefully pull her head back and stare into those mesmerizing eyes.

"I want you because you're sweet," I say quietly before I press a kiss to her cheek. "Because you're beautiful." Another kiss to her neck. "Because you're smart and generous." My lips find her exposed collarbone. "Because you're mine, princess. That's why I want you."

When I press my hips forward, she whimpers and squirms against me, her hands coming to my chest to hold on.

"What if I don't want to be yours?"

I pause, a small smirk crossing my lips. "Tell me you don't want to be mine, Katie. Tell me honestly right now that you don't want me, and I'll back off. No lying, though. We only have truth between us, baby."

Then I raise my head so I can look her in the eye. As soon as I do, I know she's not going to say those words. She might not be sure about us, but she knows she doesn't want it to stop.

"Daddy," she breathes out.

"Yeah, princess?"

She shudders, her entire body trembling against me. Her lips are swollen from nibbling on them, and her pupils are blown wide. She's practically panting. And fuck, I want to feed my cock into her open mouth.

"I need..." she whispers, her chest rising and falling rapidly. "I need something."

10
KATIE

What am I doing? I went to the edge of the cliff and leaped right off it. I've never been so bold, and I've definitely never asked for a man to make me feel good. He probably thinks I'm some desperate hussy. And that's pretty accurate because right now, I'm pretty damn desperate for him. Only him.

Grady cups my chin, his gaze burning into mine. "I like it when you call me Daddy. I want you to call me that all the time."

My pussy spasms as I nod. I like calling him Daddy, too. My body absolutely loves it. And when he talks to me like I'm a naughty Little girl, it's everything I can do not to kneel in front of him and pull his cock out to show him what a good Little girl I am. I'd never have the guts to do it, but it's the thought that counts. I should get good girl points anyway.

Slowly, we press even closer, our gazes locked on one another. I may not know as much as I'd like about Grady, but I'm confident about the important things. He has a good heart, and he's loyal. That's all I need to know.

His lips capture mine, cutting off every thought beyond how it feels when he kisses me. It's not light or quick. It's all-consuming. His air is my air. I slip my arms around his neck and lift to my tiptoes. He slides his hands to my ass and lifts me onto the counter.

I don't know where he ends and I begin. Our mouths bruise each other. Our tongues dance together, tasting, teasing, exploring. The entire time, he keeps his hands on me while he explores my body. If I were kissing any other man, I'd probably panic over all my soft spots being touched. The way Grady caresses me, though, like he can't get enough, quiets all my insecurities.

We're breathless by the time he pulls away. My nipples ache. I want him. I want this. I want to forget all my responsibilities and be careless for once.

"Grady."

"Hm? What, baby girl?"

His stiff cock brushes against my leg. It sends a thrill through me. Even hidden in his slacks, the outline is big. I'm not surprised. Grady is a confident man, and with a cock like his, I can see why.

"I think I want…"

Shaking his head, he gently cups my chin. "It's not happening tonight."

"But—"

"I said no. Believe me, baby, all I can think about right now is stripping you naked so I can kiss and lick every inch of your body. It's painful how much I want you. But what I want more is to take care of you. The only things that are going to happen are a movie, snuggles, and an early bedtime. But I'm not leaving when it's time to go to sleep."

Ugh. Why does he have to be so freaking sweet?

"You're going to be my good girl and let me feed you some dinner. I brought Italian from Vino's. Chloe said it's your favorite."

"Tell me about your parents."

My chest squeezes as I think about them. "They were wonderful. Full of life. Loved coffee. It's how they met, actually. At their favorite café. I was two when they opened Twisted Bean."

I smile sadly, finding comfort in Grady's strength as

he holds me against him. After we ate, he sent me to my room to change into some pajamas before we settled down on my bed to watch a movie. I picked the cutest short and tank top pajama set I could find. When he walked in and saw me, I thought he was going to jump my bones. Unfortunately, I was so very wrong. At least the outline of his cock pressing against his slacks made me feel a little better. He definitely wants me, but he's holding back. I find it both sweet and frustrating.

I was practically panting when he took off his suit jacket, rolled up the sleeves of his button-down shirt, and then kicked off his shoes to lie down with me. His arms are covered in tattoos. Talk about a lady boner. The man is so freaking sexy without even trying.

The movie we chose ended nearly an hour ago, but we haven't moved, and I don't want to any time soon. His arms feel like home. Something I don't want to think too deeply about.

"My dad got sick when I was six. He went through chemo and other treatments that helped prolong his life, but he was always sick. I was thirteen when he died. We'd been prepared for it, but it was still hard. My mom struggled after. It took a while before we got back on our feet. Then, right as things started settling, my mom was diagnosed with cancer. We'd thought she'd beaten it, but within a year, it returned again. She passed away nearly six months ago."

He strokes my back in silence. My eyes burn with

tears. He gives me a gentle squeeze, and they begin to fall. I wish my parents could meet Grady. They'd like him.

"So you spent most of your life taking care of your parents instead of them taking care of you," he says softly.

When I don't say anything, he kisses the top of my head. "That's going to change, baby girl. From now on, I'm going to take care of you."

My throat tightens, and it's like a weight has been lifted. I don't truly expect him to take care of me. I'm a big girl. But the idea of someone else being in control, Grady in particular, is something I can dream about for sure.

"What about your parents? Where are they?" I ask.

11
GRADY

Memories come whooshing back—ones I've tried my hardest to forget. I'll have to tell her at some point, but I hadn't planned on it so soon. She deserves to know. Maybe she'll understand why I function the way I do. Why I'm so overprotective and controlling. Why I want to take care of her and make sure she's safe all the time.

"You don't have to tell me," she says softly, stroking my chest.

I shake my head and swallow. "It's okay," I answer roughly. "It's hard to talk about, but I want you to know."

She doesn't speak. Instead, she squeezes me tighter, and it's exactly what I need.

"I was born in Ireland. My father was in the top six

of the mafia over there. One day, we were driving home, and we were ambushed. We lived in the country, and our house was several miles off the main road. Cars surrounded us from every direction. I don't even know where they came from. My younger brother was next to me, and my mom in front of him. My dad shouted for us to get out and run. So I did. I got out and sprinted as fast and hard as I could go, knowing my brother had gone the other direction with my mom."

Bile rises in my throat, and I have to take a second to breathe.

"By the time I stopped, I was deep in a forested area. I don't know how far I'd gone. It could have been a mile or more. I was only seven. Ryan was five. I hoped my mom was with him because he couldn't take care of himself. Hours passed, and I waited until it was dark before I slowly made my way back to where our car was.

"I'm not sure how long it took me. I was exhausted and scared when I finally made it." My voice is raw. and my chest is painfully tight. It's been a long time since I've spoken about my family to anyone. "They were all slaughtered in the middle of the road."

Katie lets out a sob, her fingers wrapped in my shirt. "Oh my God," she sniffles. "I'm so sorry."

I hold her closer, soaking in her warmth and sweetness. Overall, I've had a good life. I'm more than fortunate, and I have people who have my back no matter what. I've also experienced a lot of grief and ugliness. Things that have scarred my soul and turned my heart black.

Katie gives me something to live for. To look forward to. And she's so fucking good down to her core. I need some of that because I'm not so sure I have much good left in me.

"Declan's father was my uncle. When he got wind of what happened the next day, he got me on a private jet immediately and brought me to America. He raised me like his own, and I'm grateful for him. I probably would have ended up dead if I'd stayed in Ireland."

She shifts, then swings a leg over my waist and crawls on top of me, her gaze sad and her nose red from crying. When she lowers herself and hugs me with her whole body, I let out a deep breath, and a major weight lifts from my shoulders. She's like a balm for my soul.

"I'm not an easy man, baby. I need control. It helps me feel like I can keep bad things from happening. I'm going to be obsessed with your safety, and you're going to have a ridiculous number of rules surrounding it. I'll have trackers put in all your shoes, and I'll want to know where you are at all times. It will be suffocating." I close my eyes, squeezing them tight. "I guess I'm telling you this because if you think you can't handle it or don't want it, I need to know now before I become even more invested than I already am."

The last thing I want to do is give her an out. Especially this early because it's likely she'll realize how many red flags I have and run for the hills. I wouldn't blame her. I'm not fully convinced I'd let her go, but at least I'm trying to be a decent man.

Her fingers move over my ribcage. I can feel the magnetic buzz between us, even through my shirt. "I've never had anyone in my life who gave me rules and boundaries. It wasn't my parents' fault. If my dad hadn't gotten sick, I would have grown up with two loving and traditional parents, but when he was diagnosed, I had to become an adult." Her silky tone soothes my rough edges. "I think I might like you being so involved."

She sits up, her pussy pressed right against my cock. I lower my gaze to take in the sight, wishing she didn't have those damn cute pajama shorts on. Why the hell did I take sex off the table tonight? When did I become a man with good intentions? Maybe she's already rubbing off on me. What I'd really fucking like right now, though, is for her to be rubbing me off.

"I've never had this kind of relationship before," she says, then nibbles on her lip. "I've never had any relationship before. I mean, I've gone out with guys and stuff, but I've never actually had a boyfriend."

"Are you a virgin?" I blurt out. Because if she is, I need to get my dick under control real quick.

Her lips curl up into a smile as she laughs. "No. But I've only had sex twice. Well, with another person anyway."

My dick throbs. "You're saying you play with your pretty little pussy by yourself?"

Her cheeks turn bright red as she ducks her head and giggles nervously. "Um, I plead the fifth?"

Smirking, I lift my hips slightly, so she feels the full length of my erection. "New rule. No pleasuring yourself without my permission."

The gasp she makes is so dramatic that I laugh. You'd think I'd told her she couldn't eat chocolate ever again.

"That's so mean. I don't think I like that rule."

"Yeah, well, you're going to obey that rule or you're going to be punished. Besides, I never claimed to be nice."

We stare at each other, her nipples pebbling under my gaze. Fuck. I need to put her to bed. If I don't stop this, I'm going to end up fucking her all night. My girl needs sleep first.

"Time for bed, baby."

She pops her bottom lip out and sighs. "Fine. But… you're staying, right?"

"Yes, baby. I'm staying."

Relief flashes in her gaze. The feeling is mutual. I

don't care if I have to sit across the room and stare at her all night, as long as I'm near her. Not being able to get her ready for bed and watch her sleep this past week has been torture. I almost asked Cage to install cameras in her bedroom, but that might be crossing a line.

"Go potty and brush your teeth." I get to my feet and hold out my hand for her. Once she's in the bathroom, I undo my belt and remove my shirt and socks. Should I take off my pants? I have underwear on, but it might be better to have a couple of layers between us. No, fuck it. I want to be as close to her as possible, even if I'm only stripping away one more piece of clothing. Just as I set my slacks to the side, she appears in the doorway, her eyes wide as she looks me up and down.

Her tongue dips out to wet her lips, and I stifle a groan. There's no hiding my hard-on, so I don't try. It's going to be a long night, but it's also going to be so fucking worth the torture.

"Wow. You have a lot of tattoos," she murmurs.

"Aye, lass. What about you? Do you have any?"

She bites her lip. "Maybe."

Now that's surprising. My Little girl has ink on her body.

"Let Daddy see."

I wait for her to come to me. When she does, I hold my breath as she peels down the waistband of her shorts to expose her right hip. A small heart outline adorns her milky skin, and fuck me, I want my name tattooed inside of it.

"That's cute, baby. No others?"

"No. I got this when my mom was doing better. I just wanted to do something kind of naughty, so I got this."

"Well, that was definitely naughty. My naughty girl."

She giggles.

"You're also my good girl."

Her laughter turns into a wide grin. Taking her hand, I nudge her toward the bed.

"It's time to sleep."

As soon as I get under the covers with her, she snuggles up to me and sighs. "Grady."

"I prefer Daddy."

She's silent for a second. "Daddy," she whispers.

My heart pounds faster. "Yeah, baby girl?"

"I'm really glad I met you. Even if you were stalking me."

I press a kiss to her forehead, her scent lingering between us. "I'm glad I met you too, baby. And I don't know what you're talking about. Now, go to sleep."

Letting out a sigh, she fingers the silver chain I have on. "Night, Daddy," she finally says.

"Night, Little one."

It's still dark when I wake, but I can't remember the last time I felt so rested. Did I sleep all night?

Katie is sprawled over me, practically star-fished on the bed. Her weight on me is comforting. Maybe that's why I slept so well. She's also snoring, and it's adorable. I think she must have slept well, too, if she's this comfortable. That's what I was hoping for. My girl needs her rest. Especially once we have sex. I plan on wearing her out as often as possible. I'm not sure I've ever wanted to fuck someone so badly.

I lie in the dim light as the sun slowly starts to rise. This week has been a whirlwind. It feels like she's been in my life for so much longer. There's still so much I need to learn about her, but I know the most important stuff. She's strong, but she needs someone stronger to take the lead. And she needs someone to coddle and care for her because she never experienced that growing up. She also has a kind and giving heart, which has the potential to get her into trouble if she's not careful. That's why I'll have strict rules set to keep her safe.

An arm flails through the air and whacks me in the forehead as she readjusts her position. I muffle a laugh.

"What are you laughing at?" she says sleepily.

"You doing yoga in your sleep."

Her lips twitch. "I am not."

I roll onto my side to face her and gently tuck her messy hair behind her ear. "Okay, baby. Whatever you say."

She slides her fingers down my chest, teasing one of my nipples before she continues down my abs. My cock jumps from her touch. When she stops over one of my fresher scars, her gaze flits down to it.

"It's a bullet wound from a few months ago."

Her hand stills, and she looks up at me, suddenly pale. "You got shot?"

Cupping her hip in my palm, I squeeze it, loving the soft flesh. "Aye, baby. I've been shot a few times."

We lie in silence for a long beat before she takes a deep breath. "So, is this what it will be like being with you? Always worrying about you getting shot? Or killed?"

It's a valid concern. One I hate that she'll have, but I can't change my life. I need her to understand and accept the risks.

"My job is dangerous, baby. Just like being a police officer or firefighter. There are things that could happen. We do everything we can to eliminate danger, which is why I take your safety so seriously. There are no guarantees in life, but I promise that while we're here on this earth, I'll give you the best life you could ever dream of. And if anything were to ever happen to me, you'd be taken care of."

"Money doesn't mean anything to me," she says.

"I know. It's one of the reasons I adore you so much. Despite that, though, you'll have everything you could ever want or need."

Her hand starts moving again, lower and lower. I'm practically sweating by the time she reaches the waistband of my underwear. I don't know if I can resist her again. I want her more than I want my next breath.

"Katie," I growl quietly, gritting my teeth so hard it's painful. "You need to know that once we have sex, there's no turning back. I won't give you any more outs. I'll claim you and own your beautiful body. You'll be mine. Permanently. I need you to understand that."

She lingers for only a beat before she slides her hand over my fabric-covered cock. "You're right. There are no guarantees in life, and I don't want to spend mine regretting not giving you and this a chance. I want you to be my boyfriend and my Daddy."

When she squeezes my shaft, I groan. Something inside me snaps. Fuck it. She wants this, I want this, and it doesn't matter how long we've known each other.

"Let's get one thing straight, baby girl," I say as I move to hover over her with my forearms on either side of her head. "You won't be my girlfriend, and I won't be your boyfriend."

"Oh," she whispers, her eyebrows pinched.

"What we'll be is more than just boyfriend and girlfriend. You'll be mine. And I'll be yours. You won't see other men because you'll belong to me. I won't see other women because I'll belong to you. Understand what I'm saying, sweetheart?" I finish the sentence by flexing my hips so my cock presses against her core.

She whimpers and nods, her eyes glazed over. "Yes."

"That's my good girl," I praise before I lower my mouth to hers, capturing her lips with mine.

Our kiss starts off gentle and slow. She opens for me when I nudge her lips with my tongue. I've never felt so connected with someone, mind, body, soul.

When I pull back to look at her, my world is perfect. Unable to keep up the gentleness, I kiss her again, only this time, it's hard and demanding. She claws at me and wraps her legs around my waist like she needs me closer. The only way for me to get there is with my dick inside her, but we're not there yet.

"Who do you belong to, Katie-baby?" I study her face, waiting to hear it. She doesn't hesitate.

"You, Daddy. I belong to you."

Dropping my lips to her neck, I nip at the tender skin. "And I belong to you, Little girl."

She moans and throws her head back, giving me more access to her collarbone. I take my time, kissing, licking, and biting. When I reach the lace on her tank top, I tug it down, freeing her big tits. They bounce in front of me, teasing me with her dark, pebbled nipples, practically begging for my mouth. I latch onto one of them and suck, groaning as she moves her hand between us to stroke my erection.

It's intimate and desperate, and fuck, I think I'm in love with this woman.

12

KATIE

His cock throbs against my core, and it's teasing me as if it were my own fingers down there, knowing the exact right spot to touch.

"Holding back on you has been torture, princess." He presses his mouth to me again, his tongue exploring, demanding, owning me. I want to give him everything. All of me. Maybe I've lost my mind, but I trust him not to hurt me.

I move my hips, needing to get closer. What I really want is him inside of me, stretching me around his thickness. And it's freaking girthy. I never knew a dick could be so big.

"Are you on birth control, baby?"

The question catches me off guard. Leave it to him to remember the safety stuff. "Yes. I have an implant."

He stares at me for a moment before he nods. "Might need to get that taken out soon," he murmurs.

Wait. What? Is he saying he wants to get me pregnant? With his baby? Huh. I don't hate the thought of my tummy getting big and round with a baby that looks like him. Wow. I'm losing my mind.

Sliding his hand between us, he slips his fingers into my shorts and panties and yanks them down just enough so he can tease my clit.

As soon as he touches me, I swear, sparks crackle, and I cry out, bucking against him. It won't take much for me to shatter. I've never felt so needy. So ready. So wet.

"Daddy," I whisper urgently.

We stare at each other while he draws lazy circles around my sensitive nub. Oh my God. This is what ecstasy is. Pure pleasure, almost to the point of glorious pain.

"You sound so beautiful when you cry my name like that."

A shiver runs through me. My lips fall back into a lazy smile, my hips jerking with every stroke he gives.

"You make me feel beautiful."

He stares at me intently. I've never felt so seen by someone.

"That's because you are, princess. I hate that I've been on this earth all this time without knowing you. You're a fucking gift, Katie. One I'll cherish."

I open my mouth, but he silences me with a kiss. He continues to play with me while I move my hands down his inked torso to his boxer briefs. Desperate, I push them down over his round ass, letting his cock spring free against my thigh. Unable to resist, I grasp it and moan when it twitches in my hand. It's so long and thick and smooth. I'm not even looking at it, but I already know it's beautiful.

"I want to fuck you bare, baby. I'm clean. I was just tested last month and haven't been with anyone since."

Bobbing my head, I whimper, my orgasm building, getting closer and closer to explosion. "I'm clean, too. I haven't been with anyone in a long time."

His pupils dilate. "Good. And you'll never be with another man again. Only me, baby girl. Only me."

There's something so concrete in his words. It's a promise.

Our movements turn wild and erratic as he yanks my shorts and panties farther down my legs. I use my toes to push his underwear down his. When I glance between us and get a look at his dick, I swallow heavily.

"You're really big," I say breathlessly.

He chuckles and pulls my tank up and over my head, leaving me completely nude before him. "I'll be gentle. At first."

My tummy does a little nervous flip, but I nod. I trust him. Grady will take care of me.

"You're so wet, baby girl. Is that for me? Were you wet for me each time I came into the coffee shop?"

Fudge. Was I that obvious?

He smirks. "That's okay. You don't have to answer, shy girl. I can tell by the flush on your cheeks and the way your pussy is twitching against my fingers."

Poker is obviously not my game.

My train of thought dissolves into thin air as he lines the head of his cock up to my pussy and strokes it along my slit. I'm so ready for him. I've never been so wet. Not even when I've pleasured myself.

"Look at me, princess. I want to see those beautiful eyes when I slide into your tight cunt."

I let my head fall back onto the mattress. We stare at each other. No words are spoken as he reaches down and fists his cock, lining it up to my center. As soon as he nudges forward, it pinches. Goosebumps rise all over my body, and I widen my thighs as much as I can.

"I don't like hurting you," he says through clenched teeth.

"Please don't stop." I rest my hands on his tattooed chest and try to lift my hips to urge him forward.

"You're killing me, baby. Stop moving. I'm going to come before I even get inside you if you don't stop fucking wiggling."

A smile tugs at my lips, but I obey, and he rewards me with another small thrust forward. I cry out, my fingers curling into his skin.

Little by little, he inches into me, both of us panting. Sweat coats our skin by the time his hips meet the inside of my thighs. My heart pounds, and butterflies flutter in my tummy. I'm consumed by him physically and emotionally. I have to blink several times, not wanting the tears burning my eyes to fall. That would surely be a mood killer for him, even though they're ones of happiness.

"You're everything, sweetheart. Everything I've ever hoped for. Prayed for. Dreamed of," he murmurs softly.

The moment is delicate. Meaningful. Intimate. I think both of us are experiencing life-changing emotions. I know I am.

He pulls out and thrusts back in slowly, the ridge of his cock gliding against that spot inside me that I've only read about and never felt. Not even when I'd tried to find it with toys.

"Ohhhh."

For several seconds, we move in slow motion, savoring every stroke, but like a light switch flips, we turn desperate. I claw at his chest and dig my heels into his hard ass, wanting to pull him as close to me as possible. He fucks me harder and faster, leaning down every so often to bite at my breasts and suck on my pebbled nipples.

"Fuck," he growls.

"Oh, God!" I cry out, the pressure on my clit

growing with every passing second.

"You need to come, baby? You need your Daddy to make you come all over his dick?"

Without waiting for an answer, he reaches between us and finds my clit. As soon as he applies pressure and then thrusts, I scream. Waves of pleasure crash through me, spreading through my entire body as my pussy convulses.

I may not walk tomorrow, but it'll be worth it. This will all be worth it. He pulls his hand from between us and brings his first two fingers to his mouth, sucking them clean.

"Fuck," he growls. "I should have eaten your pussy first because it tastes like heaven."

He buries his hand in my hair at the base of my neck and closes his fist around it, giving me a bite of pain that quickly morphs into pleasure.

"You're going to come again, baby. We're going to come together."

Panic rushes through me. I can't come again. I can't believe I was able to once. That's never happened with a man before. Only by myself.

"I can't."

"You can, baby. And you will."

Anxiety floods me, a heavy weight settling in the pit of my tummy. I don't want to disappoint him. I can fake it, I guess. I've done it before. It sort of breaks my heart that I'll have to do it with Grady because I feel so much for him, but I don't want to make him feel bad or inadequate because I won't come again.

He lowers his body so his chest is pressed against my breasts, and his elbows are resting above each of my shoulders, his hands buried in my hair. His mouth hovers near the shell of my ear.

I wrap my arms around him and gently scrape my fingernails down his back. At least I don't have to look him in the face while I fake it.

"God sent you to me to be mine." He thrusts slow but deep. "Mine to take care of. Mine to protect. Mine to love. Mine to fuck." This time, he thrusts harder, almost painfully hard, yet I want more. "Mine. You're mine."

A shiver runs through me, and he tightens his fingers in my hair as he starts fucking me ruthlessly. Our skin slaps together, and the sound of my wetness fills the space around us. Suddenly, my entire body explodes. From head to toe, I detonate, screaming as an orgasm tears through me, shaking me down to the core.

Grady's movements become erratic, and then we're both crying out as he climaxes with me, his cock throbbing inside my pulsing pussy.

Holy hell.

We collapse back on the mattress, unable to move. My eyes are so heavy, I can't keep them open a second longer. I don't need to. Daddy's here. He'll take care of me.

"Baby, sit up and take a drink."

I make a noise of protest and shake my head. Opening my eyes is the last thing on my to-do list. Right now, my top priority is to take a two-day nap to recover from those orgasms.

"Katie-baby, sit up." His voice is deeper this time. Sterner. Sexier. My clit does a little dance. Then he adds, "Do I need to count to three, Little girl?"

Both of my eyes pop open, and I glare at him. "You're not being very nice. I was resting, which you always seem to be encouraging me to do."

He chuckles and sits on the edge of the bed. "So, my girl gets sassy after she's freshly fucked, huh?"

My cheeks heat so much they could probably pop popcorn.

"While I do want you to rest, you need some hydration. If sitting up to have some water is too difficult for you, I can bring it in a baby bottle next time, and you can drink it that way."

Say what now?

"I can sit up," I blurt out.

The corners of his mouth twitch as he holds one of my pink cups to my lips. "Then show Daddy what a good girl you can be and take some drinks."

I watch him as I gulp down the freezing cold water. He's right. I do need this. My throat is raw from all the screaming.

Finally, I pull away and sigh. "Thank you."

This was definitely not how I planned the night to go. Grady here, naked, stopping me from getting anything done. I also can't believe how relaxed I am about it all. I have so much to do. A cake to bake. Accounting to catch up on. But what I'm doing right now feels so right.

He studies me closely, his gaze penetrating and serious. "Let me take care of you, princess."

A lump slides up my throat. All my life, I've taken care of others. I haven't had much of a choice in the matter. I don't regret the time I spent caring for my parents. But I used to wonder what it would be like to be the one on the receiving end.

And here is Grady. Offering me just that.

It sounds like heaven. Like everything I could hope for. But what happens when he moves on from me? Surely, he's not the kind of man to settle down. And with a girl like me who thinks a night in with coffee and a book sounds like the best time ever? Yeah, no.

He'd be bored as hell. It wouldn't take long. Then what? I'd be back to where I am now.

Passing up a chance to spend time with a man like Grady would be tragic, though. I think I'd always regret it. If anything, this might be the exciting part of my life that I tell stories about when I'm old and gray. Besides, if he keeps giving orgasms like he did a little while ago, it will be well worth the heartbreak that follows.

"I'd like that," I whisper, my fingers smoothing over Pancake's fur.

He slowly reaches out and cups my chin, giving me a feather-light kiss on the lips. "I know you're afraid, Katie. I am, too, but probably for other reasons. We both need to take a leap of faith and see what happens because I'm fairly certain this thing between us is going to be the most beautiful thing in the world."

What reason would he have to be scared? He has everything. Money. Power. Lots of guns and possibly even some grenades. He's right, though. I'm terrified.

Take a leap of faith.

My parents always used to say that. Hearing it from Grady is like hearing their voices again, reminding me. Maybe it's a sign, or maybe I'm sex-high and hearing things, but I'm going to choose to take the chance.

I nod and lean forward so my head rests on his shoulder. "Okay."

He twists, plucking me up from my spot on the bed

and sitting me on his lap. At least I have a T-shirt on. He's completely naked, and his cock is hard again, pressing into my ass.

"We need to go over some rules," he says firmly.

Rules? What is it with these men and rules? It seems like they're handing them out all the time. Declan added a rule to Cali's list last night over dinner. It was the most interesting thing to watch as they discussed it, and she finally agreed. No one at the table even seemed to blink an eye.

"I don't need rules."

His chest rumbles, and his cock twitches, sending a rush of excitement through me. Unable to resist, I grind against him, then yelp when he swats my thigh.

"This is serious, Little one. You do need rules, and you will follow them, or you will find yourself in trouble. Almost all your rules will be for your safety and health, which I will take very seriously. A few will be for my own personal pleasure. You're not dating a normal man, baby."

I grin. "Are you actually a robot?"

He pauses and narrows his eyes, but the corners of his lips twitch upward. "Very funny, Little girl."

Letting out a sigh, I give him my attention. The way his shoulders are tensed, I sense this is a serious topic for him. Though, I don't know how I feel about having rules set for me. I don't think I had any when I was a kid. Then again, I wasn't able to do much kid stuff anyway.

"When it comes to your safety, I don't take it lightly. I'll need to know where you are at all times. You will not go to any bars, clubs, wineries, or anywhere that serves alcohol without me or a bodyguard."

My mouth falls open, and I scrunch my face. "A bodyguard? Why would I need one of those?"

His expression is so serious that it's almost scary. He's not joking. But I don't understand why I would need a bodyguard. I'm just me.

"Baby, my life is dangerous. There are always risks involved with dating a man in the mafia. We have many enemies, and sometimes things happen. Our first priority is always to protect you girls."

Holy crap. "That's why that guy came into the coffee shop with Chloe when she was alone."

"Yes. The girls have round-the-clock protection details. Like I said, our girls—and that includes you now—are our top priority."

"Yeah, but they're all married to their guys and living there. You're just dating me."

His face drops into a scowl, and he shifts me roughly so I'm straddling him. He keeps his gaze on mine but moves his hands to my hips, gripping me tightly. "Baby, I'm not dating you."

Wow. Okay. Why does that feel like a total stab to my heart?

"Dating is for people who don't have a plan. Dating is for jerks who aren't man enough to make a commitment. We're not fucking dating, princess. You're mine. Your body, soul, and heart. They're all mine, and I'm all yours. I'm going to marry you one day. Which means you're part of my family, and it's my responsibility and pleasure to protect you. I can't be with you all the time, so when I can't, you will have a bodyguard with you."

I blink slowly, trying to process all that. Marry? He wants to marry me? We've known each other for a week. I was worried it was too soon for sex, but he's already talking about marriage.

"Baby," he murmurs, and I let my eyes focus on him. "I'm a possessive man, and I'm over the top. I'm going to drive you up the wall, and you're probably going to want to shoot me with my own gun some days, but I will give you the best life. We're not getting married tomorrow, so let's not focus on that right now. I want you to know my intentions, though. Understand?"

"Yes."

He beams and nods. "My good girl. Next rule."

All my tension drains away, and I let out a small giggle. Always focused on the rules.

"What happens if I break one?"

His fingers move gently up and down my thighs as he stares at me. "If you break a rule, you will be disciplined. Usually spanked by my hand, belt, or a paddle. Depending on my mood, I might decide to put a plug in your bottom and make you keep it in for a few hours."

My eyes bulge as wetness gathers between my legs. I try to squeeze my thighs together, but his bulk is in the way. As if he knows, a satisfied smile spreads over his lips.

"Like that idea, lass? Of Daddy lubing up your naughty bottom hole and pushing a thick plug inside?"

My entire body heats. My nipples could cut glass from how hard they are. He notices them and strokes a hand over one of the sensitive buds.

"Has anyone ever touched you back there, Katie-baby?" His voice is practically a purr.

"No," I pant.

"Good. That pleases me. I'll be the first and last man to take your asshole. Mm, fuck." The purr becomes a growl.

I shudder at the thought of his long, thick cock inside my ass.

"You like that," he says.

"I…I, um, I'm not sure. I've read books about it, and I like reading them, but I'm scared it will hurt."

His entire expression gentles, and he cups my face between his hands. "I would never do anything to intentionally harm you. When we get to that point together, Daddy will make sure you're ready so it doesn't hurt. Okay?"

"Okay. Thank you."

"When I discipline you, it will never be to harm you either. Sometimes, it will hurt, and you'll cry, but it will be temporary, and you'll have a safeword."

Nodding, I study his face, and everything inside me melts. Is it possible to fall in love with someone after a week?

13

GRADY

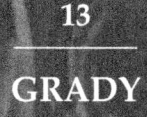

I knew he was bad news. The name sounded so familiar. Which is why I'm standing in front of Calvin Dunlap's office with Bash, Killian, and Cage Black at my side. I don't really know why Cage is here, but he said he wanted to join us, then gave me the most evil fucking grin I've ever seen, so there was no way in hell I was going to say no.

After my conversation with Kieran about Calvin, I reached out to Cage and asked him to dig up some info about the real estate agent. Cage came up with a lot of shit that I'm sure Calvin hoped would never be brought to light.

The young, pretty receptionist stands when the four of us walk into the pretentious office, her face going pale. There's no doubt we're intimidating. We're all over six feet tall, have hand tattoos, and wear suits that cost more than most cars. Except for Cage. I've only seen him dressed up once. It was weird. Like today, he usually wears jeans, T-shirts, and some worn-in boots that I think are meant to look that way. I don't think the guy is into fashion, but then again, I'm also pretty sure he's a psychopath, so who knows what shit he's into.

"Um, hello," she says so quietly I barely hear her. The poor thing is shaking like a leaf. I wish we could reassure her that we'd never harm her, but I'm doubtful it would do any good.

"Hello. I need to speak with Calvin Dunlap. Can you point me to his office?" I ask.

She swallows and stares up at me for a few seconds before we're interrupted.

"Doll-face, you gave me the wrong report."

I turn toward the voice and glare. Calvin Fucking Dunlap. Past charges of fraud. Theft. A handful of other misdemeanor crimes. All of which he's somehow gotten dropped. All by the same judge.

He pauses mid-step. When his gaze lands on Cage, his eyes bulge.

"Hey, old *friend*," Cage says with a grin.

Calvin backs up, but Cage follows, and we go with him until the five of us are inside a large office. Killian closes the door and locks it.

"W-what are you doing here?" Calvin asks, wiping sweat from his forehead.

Cage shrugs, smiling at the asshole. "I'm just here for fun, and I'm having a fucking blast, man. How about you?"

I look from Cage to Calvin and back again. Okay, so obviously they know each other. Cage didn't mention that. Whatever their history, it's not good.

"Good, man. Good. Real good. Yep," Calvin squeaks out.

Shaking my head, I charge toward him. "You've been working with my girl, Katie, on selling her parents' house."

Something flashes in Calvin's eyes before he nods. "Right, right. Yeah, the old ranch house."

"Yeah. You no longer work for her. As of today, you'll never speak to her again. The list of bullshit you gave her to do to fix up the house, what the fuck was that all about?"

"I was just trying to help her get the most money for the house, man. She's trying to pay off her parents' medical bills," he answers quickly.

I take another step closer, my irritation prickling the back of my neck. "Trying to get top dollar so you could line your fucking pockets. We pulled some financials on you, Calvin. Seems you've been getting a really high commission off your sales lately."

He shakes his head. "I don't know what you're talking about."

Bash scoffs. "Like hell you don't, asshole. You

know exactly what the fuck you're doing. And it seems you must be blowing a judge on a regular basis to get all these fucking charges dropped over and over. You've been doing sleazy shit ever since you were a teen."

Cage snorts. "I'll say. Ole Calvin, or as I know him, Walter Boris Dunlap the Third. How the fuck did you come up with the name Calvin? You decided to give yourself a different name, and you fucking chose Calvin? Shows what a fucking idiot you still are. But I guess when your father is a judge, you can do whatever the fuck you want, am I right, *Waltie*?"

What the fuck?

"Walter's parents fostered me for a few months," Cage adds. "And boy, oh, boy, Waltie here always made me feel right at home. In between the times he was terrorizing neighborhood animals, of course."

Oh, shit.

Calvin's skin turns so pale it's almost scary. It's also fucking hilarious.

Strolling forward, I give the prick a shove, then grab him by the throat before he falls on his ass. "I don't give a fuck who you are or who you know; you're going to stay away from Katie. Cage might have let you live despite his hatred for you, but I won't if you cross me. This is your only warning."

I release him with another shove, sending him

flailing backward into a wall. I'm surprised by how quickly he recovers and starts to straighten his suit.

"Whatever you say, man," Calvin mumbles as he brushes off some invisible lint.

God, the guy is slimy. It makes me sick to think he's ever been alone with Katie. I need to make that one of her rules. No being alone with any man but me or one of ours.

"I could have gone a fucking lifetime without ever seeing your ugly ass, and yet here you are, in Seattle of all fucking places, and I'm regretting letting you live. Won't be so lucky next time, Dunlap. I suggest you keep one eye over your shoulder because your time is coming," Cage says calmly, then smiles so fucking wickedly that even I get goosebumps.

Whatever Calvin did to piss off Cage, it must have been good. I'm shocked the guy is still alive. Cage isn't known for being forgiving.

Feeling like I got my point across, I stride out of the office and don't stop until the four of us are near the SUVs.

Turning to Cage, I narrow my eyes. "You knew who he was and decided to keep that little piece of information to yourself?"

Cage shrugs like it's no big deal. "It wasn't important for your situation."

"Why is the piece of shit still living?" Killian demands.

"Because it was more fun breaking his arm in three places with my bare hands and watching his dream of being a star baseball player go down the drain one shitty hit at a time," Cage answers with a smirk. "Besides, I went to juvie six months later, sentenced by his father. That's when I was recruited onto my team, and I had to leave my past in the past. I hadn't seen him again until today."

Damn.

"Anyway, this was fun. I have shit to do. I'll be in touch." Cage salutes as he heads toward his vehicle.

Killian, Bash, and I glance at one another and shake our heads before we climb into the SUV. Cage is a mystery, but we really fucking like him.

Bash turns his attention to me. "What's the plan now?"

I drive toward *my* realtor's office. "Now, I figure out how to get Katie to move in with me. Do you think it's too soon to ask?"

Bash laughs. "Why would you ask? Just move her shit to your house and cancel her lease. Decision made. Boom."

Killian turns to look back at Bash. "Dude, how the fuck did you turn out like this? It's like you see a line and dance right past it every time."

Snorting, I nod. "It's true. But I do like the way you're thinking."

"Jesus Christ. Are you seriously thinking of taking

advice from Bash?" Killian scrubs a hand over his face and shakes his head.

I shrug. It's not the worst idea I've ever heard. Katie belongs with me, turning my house into our home. She needs a bedtime and someone to take care of her. I can't do that like I want to if she isn't living under my roof.

Killian sighs. "I never thought I'd be the sanest person in this group."

Bash slaps his shoulder. "Just remember Declan stalked Cali for half a year before they got together, so I think we're all sane compared to him."

It's kind of true. I've been lightly stalking Katie, but nowhere close to the degree that Declan did with Cali.

However it happens, Katie belongs with me. Whether she's ready or not. I am, so she needs to get on board.

As soon as I walk into Twisted Bean, I know something is wrong before I even lay eyes on her. The air is different. Sadder. Heavier.

When I pass the espresso machine and finally see her behind it, making a drink, my chest squeezes. She looks exhausted. And her normally sparkling eyes are dim.

"Baby girl," I murmur so only she can hear.

She looks up, and her shoulders drop like she's been waiting to see me all day. "Hi," she whispers.

I watch as she caps the coffee, sets it out for the waiting customer, and then meets me at the end of the counter. Right away, I pull her into my arms.

"What's wrong with my girl?" I ask before pressing a kiss to her forehead.

Letting out a deep sigh, she looks up at me. "Just a busy day, and I got an email from my real estate agent telling me he wouldn't be able to work with me any longer because of scheduling conflicts. Whatever that means. I didn't like him anyway, but now I need to find a new one, and I don't have time to start all over. The insurance company is constantly pestering me for payment. They've been pretty patient up until now. I thought the house would be sold already, and then I could pay them off. Or mostly off anyway."

My heart and cock both ache for her but in different ways. She's so small compared to me. I'd never think of her as weak because it's obvious how strong my girl is, but fuck, she's struggling. As her Daddy, I need to step in before she breaks.

"Breathe, baby girl. We'll handle all of this together. It's not all on you anymore."

She pushes against me and shakes her head. "Grady."

Oh no. Fuck no. She's not going to push me away and feed me a line of bullshit about whatever trash she's telling herself.

"You don't want to get involved with me. I'm a mess."

Yep. Straight fucking garbage.

I look around, noting one of her employees cleaning a table, then grab Katie by the wrist and lead her toward the back room. I haven't seen the entire shop yet, but there's got to be somewhere private where I can make things perfectly fucking clear to her.

To the left is a small but organized office. I pull her in and close the door behind us.

"Grady, what are you doing?" she asks, her eyes wide and her tone tinged with fear.

Ignoring her, I spin her toward the desk and push her down roughly so her chest is resting on a pile of papers. Then I smack her ass.

"What am I doing, baby girl? I'm teaching you a lesson. That's what Daddy is doing. Because you think you have to take on the world all alone, you're pushing yourself to your limits. That's going to end, right here, right now." I smack her ass again, and she yelps. "When I sank my cock deep into your pussy, no condom, nothing between us but our souls, and told you that you were mine, I meant every fucking word of it. That means your problems are my problems, and you're mine to take care of. You're not allowed to push me away, Katie-baby."

I smack each cheek a few times, though I doubt it hurts all that much over her jeans. She still jumps in surprise.

"You belong to me, Little girl. I'm not Grady to you. I'm Daddy."

She's breathing hard, but she doesn't agree with me, and it makes my cock harden even more. She's testing me. Pushing me. Too bad for her and her round ass, she's going to find out this Daddy doesn't back down.

"Unbutton your jeans," I command.

"What?" she tries to rise from the desk, but I hold her down.

"Unbutton your jeans. If I have to tell you again, I'll use my belt instead of just my hand for this spanking."

"You can't spank me here," she whines, though it isn't forceful.

"I can spank you anywhere I want. One."

"What?" she asks, looking back at me in confusion.

"Two." I raise my eyebrows at her, and she jumps into action, undoing her jeans.

Once she's done, I tuck my hand around the waistband and yank them—and her underwear—down, baring her ass to me. There's only a slight pink hue on her skin where I've already spanked her.

"Have you changed your mind about wanting me, baby girl?"

She quickly shakes her head, and I start to pepper her bottom with my hand.

"Ouch! Oh, God. That hurts!" she cries out softly.

"It's supposed to hurt, baby. It's meant to teach you a lesson, which apparently you need if you think there's a chance in hell I'm going to walk away from you. And putting yourself down? Saying you're a mess? That's definitely not allowed. That's one of your rules. No negative self-talk."

"I wasn't—" She yelps. "Owwie! Daddy…"

Now we're getting somewhere. Too bad for her, this is only the start of her punishment.

14

KATIE

My butt is on fire, yet he keeps spanking me. Tears burn my eyes and worry over anyone hearing us disappears, replaced with a swell of emotions bubbling to the surface.

"You're not alone anymore, Katie. I'm right here. I can take a lot off your plate if you'll just let me. You don't have to do everything anymore."

A sob lodges in my throat. It feels like my heart is cracking into pieces. "Why would you want to take all of this on?" I say as my tears start to fall.

He pauses a second, then spanks each cheek once, harder than before. "Because I care about you. I watch you and see the kindness and selflessness pouring out of you. It's one of my favorite things about you. But it's also something that needs to be managed because you're not putting yourself first. So, guess what? I'm going to put you first."

I squeeze my eyes shut and try to clamp my lips together so he doesn't hear me as I break. The sadness I've been holding in for so long bursts free. My tears soak the papers under my face.

"I'm just so tired," I sob.

"I know, baby girl," he murmurs, then starts to spank me again. "We're going to change that. I won't allow you to push me away. I've been patient, but now it's time for me to take control. And you're going to be my good Little girl and let me, aren't you?"

Can I? I want to, so badly. I'm scared. What's the worst that could happen? He could break my heart. He could die. I don't know if I can handle losing another person I love. Oh my God. I can't possibly love him already.

He pauses and rubs my ass, soothing some of the sting as I continue to cry.

"It's time to let go, Katie-baby. It's time to let Daddy take care of you. Yeah?"

Sniffling, I shift my eyes to him. He's staring down at me as he strokes my butt. There are so many what-ifs, but I'll regret it if I don't see where this goes.

Take a leap of faith.

"Yes, Daddy."

He watches me for several seconds before giving a sharp nod. Then he starts spanking me hard and fast, and my tears pour out of me as I kick my feet and struggle against his hold.

"This is what happens when you try to push Daddy away. I won't allow it, baby."

His reassurances heal something inside of me. I know my parents couldn't help getting sick and dying, but in a way, it felt like they abandoned me.

"I'm sorry," I cry out. "I'm sorry, Daddy."

He stops, gently pulls me up, and wraps me in his arms. "You're not alone anymore. Whatever's going on, you need to talk to me. I have a lot of resources."

I nod and clutch onto him for dear life as he slowly and carefully pulls up my panties and jeans, then buttons them for me. I'm glad I skipped makeup this morning because otherwise, I'd be a total mess.

He wipes my cheeks with his thumbs. "I want you to write down the name of the insurance company for me. I'll reach out to my realtor and ask her to get your parents' house up for sale right away. Are you sure you want to sell it? Is it the house you grew up in?"

Sniffling, I shake my head. "I don't care about the house. My mom only kept it for as long as she did because she wanted to die in the same place my dad did. The house never meant anything to us. It's this shop that means the most. I grew up here. When they were opening it, they couldn't afford employees, so they worked non-stop, and I was always here too. But if I don't pay off the medical bills within thirty days, they're threatening to put a lien on the shop." A sob breaks loose again. "I can't lose Twisted Bean. It's all I have left of my parents."

He tightens his hold on me and shakes his head. "You're not going to lose anything. Daddy won't let it happen. Write down the name of the insurance company."

I take a step back and look up at him. "What are you going to do?"

"I'm going to handle it. Trust me, baby."

It might be naïve of me to trust him already, but I do. "This isn't your problem to deal with."

His eyes turn stormy. "Do we need to revisit the part where I pull your pants and panties down and you get your bottom spanked? You're mine, baby. Which means your problems are mine. So I will deal with them, and you'll be a good girl and let me."

Yikes. Stern Grady is…hot. Sheesh. I've seen him be a bit firm and bossy, but right now, he's absolutely not messing around.

With a sigh, I nod and grab a scrap of paper from the desk. When I hand it over, he cups my face and leans down to kiss me.

"That's my good girl."

A shiver runs down my spine right to my pussy. Good girl. I like being his good girl.

"I want you to stay with me tonight," he says. "What do you need from your apartment?"

My eyes nearly pop right out of the sockets. No way is he going to my apartment to rummage through my drawers. I'd be mortified if he found my footie pajamas. Or Thor.

"Oh, um, I'll run home after work and grab some stuff," I blurt out.

He stares at me as the corners of his lips slowly slide into a smile. "Afraid I might see your little pink vibrator, baby? Daddy already saw it when you were in the bathroom."

When my mouth drops open, he chuckles. "I wanted to know more about my girl."

"You looked in my drawers?"

He shrugs. "If you're expecting an apology, I'm not giving one. When it comes to you, I have no boundaries."

The black Escalade I've seen over the past week comes to mind. No. There's no way that was him. Stalking is over the top. Even if the idea of it makes me feel hot all over. God, I need help.

"I'll go get some stuff after work and then come over," I reply.

"Okay, baby. If you insist. Bring the vibrator, though. And several changes of clothes."

Cocking my head, I scrunch my face. "You said you wanted me to stay the night. Why do I need more than one change of clothes?"

That panty-melting smirk appears on his face again,

and he leans down to brush his lips over mine. "Because once I have you under my roof, I probably won't ever let you leave again."

Somehow, that feels more like a promise than a threat. I laugh anyway because, obviously, he's joking.

His phone dings several times. He scowls at it, then slides it back into his pocket.

"I should get back to work."

He peers down at me, frowns, then runs his index finger along my jaw. "I don't want to leave you after punishing you."

I don't want him to leave, either. I want to curl up in his lap and snuggle while he holds me, but I can't tell him that. He's a busy man. Surely, he has things to do.

"How soon before you can be off?" he asks. "I'll wait for you."

"You don't need to wait for me. I was off an hour ago, but I was going to stay until close so I could give Tom some extra pastries I made."

He narrows his gaze. "Who the fuck is this Tom guy? Why is he so important to you?"

My tummy flutters, and part of me wants to giggle. I like jealous Grady. It might be unhealthy to like having someone so possessive and obsessive, but I think it's exactly what I need. It's also what I crave.

"Tom is a long-time customer. He's like seventy years old. My parents were friends with him, and he still comes by almost every night at closing. I give him hot coffee and pastries. I don't want him to go hungry."

He stares down at me, seeming to consider my words. "And he's homeless?"

I nod. "Yes. I've offered to let him sleep in the coffee shop on numerous occasions, but he always turns me down. Anyway, I made his favorite scone."

The way his eyes turn hard again is adorable. Not that I'll tell him I think so because the last thing I want to do is hurt the man's ego.

"You're making another man his favorite scones?" he asks like he can't even fathom the thought.

"Did you miss the part about him being almost seventy?" I giggle and roll my eyes.

"Don't roll your eyes at me, Little girl. I don't think I like you cooking for another man. Maybe I need to meet this Tom guy."

Shit. This is backfiring quickly. I might like Grady being a bit jealous, but there have to be some boundaries.

Then, he smirks and winks at me. Oh. Ohhhh. He was joking.

"I trust you, baby girl. But, he's safe?"

Nodding, I smile. "Yes. Tom is safe. He's just about as protective as you are."

That makes him relax his shoulders. "Nobody will be as protective of you as I am. I'm glad he looks out for you, though."

"Go back to work. I'll be at your house in a few hours."

He frowns. "I don't want to leave you. Especially after a punishment."

The cracks in my heart start to heal. Why is he so amazing?

"I'm fine. I promise. I'm really happy right now, actually. I think I needed that."

Letting out a sigh, he brushes his thumb over my cheek. "I want you to let me know when you leave here, when you get to your place, and when you're on your way to my house. Understand?"

It's probably not healthy, but I love how over the top he is.

"Yes, Daddy. I understand."

"That's my good girl."

Why, yes. Yes, I am his good girl.

15

GRADY

Whoever the hell this Tom guy is, he's about to have a come-to-Jesus moment. I don't give a fuck if he's seventy or homeless or the Lord and Savior himself. Katie is mine, and I'm going to protect her by any means necessary.

I've been sitting outside Twisted Bean for the past half hour, waiting for this guy to show. Why would he come by every night? That's suspicious. I'm not a trusting guy. It's not in my nature. But when it comes to my girl, I'm even less so.

Off to the left, movement catches my eye. Sure enough, a rough-looking older man with a cart makes his way toward the shop. It looks like he hasn't had a haircut or a shave in years. His clothes have definitely seen better days. The average person would probably cross the road to avoid the guy, but they don't know any better. Most people just assume if someone is homeless, it's because they have a substance problem.

I don't think that's Tom's issue. He's too proud to sleep in Katie's shop, and he walks with his shoulders held high. My guess is he's former military. A soldier who came home and wasn't able to get the resources he needed to live as a civilian. I could be wrong, but something in my gut tells me I'm spot on.

When I get out of the SUV and slam the door closed, he turns to look at me. He's very aware of his surroundings. Definitely military.

As I approach, he studies me, not shying away like most men would.

"I was wondering how long it would take for you to introduce yourself to me," he says firmly, his voice gravelly.

I come to a stop in front of him, my spine tensing. Either Katie told him about me, or he's been keeping an eye on me.

"Why do you visit Katie every day?" I ask.

His gray eyes sparkle as he glances toward the shop. Then he lets out a slow exhale. "Because I'm a man who follows through on my promises."

My eyebrows shoot up. Now, I'm confused *and* intrigued. "What promises?"

He turns his attention back toward me. "The real question that needs answering is: What are your intentions with Katie?"

There are very few things that surprise me anymore. In my short time on earth, I've lived a thousand lives and seen things I wish I never had. Yet, this man is being protective of my woman, and I suddenly want to thank him.

"To marry her. Your turn. What promises?"

We stare at each other for a beat before he brings his weathered hand up to his beard to scratch his chin. "Her father. He asked me to keep an eye on his girls before he died. I promised I would."

Narrowing my gaze, I cock my head. "Forgive me for being skeptical, but why would he ask you to do that? How did you know each other?"

Tom smiles softly. "When Katie's parents opened the shop, her mom was trying different pastry recipes. She saw me passing and asked me to try one. I think she just felt bad for me and used it as an excuse to feed me. The pastries were terrible. Surprised I didn't die of intestinal bleeding after eating them." He chuckles and shakes his head. "She got better over time once she figured out how to tell flour and sugar apart. One night, she was at the shop baking alone. When she was going out to her car, someone attacked her and tried to rob her."

"Tried?" I ask slowly.

"I was there. I knew she was alone in the shop, so I stayed close. I liked her husband. He was a good man. Good to his wife and daughter. So it felt right to keep an eye out. That night, once I got her calmed down and we called her husband, the three of us became friends. He offered me coffee and pastries for life because I saved her."

My chest squeezes as I stare at this man. He keeps an eye on my girl to keep her safe.

"Marine?" I ask on a hunch.

"Retired."

I nod, flexing my jaw several times. "I have the best intentions for Katie. I'm in love with her."

The words feel right as I say them, but I blink several times as the realization hits.

I love her.

He narrows his gaze. "Seems kind of quick to be declaring your love. You've known her for what, a week?"

A single chuckle rolls up from my chest. "Yeah. I know it seems fast, but I knew the second I saw her."

Tom runs his fingers through his beard. "You can keep her safe with the life you lead?"

I don't know how he knows I'm in the mafia, but he does. I respect him even more now. He might be homeless, but he's smart and resourceful.

"Yes, sir. I can."

My phone buzzes, and I ignore yet another message from Sharleen. I'm going to have to send her a blunt reply telling her to leave me the fuck alone since she doesn't seem to understand the nicer ones I've sent telling her I'm not interested.

When I look back at Tom, he sighs and starts pushing his cart toward the shop again. "You hurt her, and I'll kill you. The only other people I've ever considered family are gone, and she's all I have left. I have no one else to live for."

Warmth spreads throughout me, and a slow smile stretches my lips. He's clearly dismissing me as he walks away.

"Yes, sir," I say, loud enough for him to hear.

I wasn't expecting things to go this way, but suddenly, I'm a huge fan of Tom.

"I'D LIKE you to stop calling and texting me."

She scoffs dramatically through the phone. "You don't mean that. Listen, let's go out again. I'll make it so good for you. We could have so much fun together, Grady."

Bile rises in my throat. The mere thought of being with another woman besides Katie sickens me. I will never allow another woman to touch me in that way.

"I'm going to pass on that, Sharleen. I'm with someone else."

If she gasps any louder, I'm going to put a bullet in my head. Apparently, being rejected is completely shocking to her.

"You're with someone else? We just went out two weeks ago. How is that going to look when I tell my friends? They've been so excited to meet you."

I roll my eyes. "Yeah, I've met someone since. Anyway, I need to go. Good luck."

Before she can make another noise, I end the call and shake my head. "Jesus," I murmur.

Ronan chuckles from the doorway. "Who knew you were such a popular guy with the ladies?"

Pocketing my phone, I glance up at him and smirk. "Well, welcome back. If I didn't know any better, I'd think you were moving to Ireland."

"Fuck off," he says as he strolls into the sitting room toward the bar. "Was that the girl from the influencer party who was practically rubbing her tits all over you to mark her territory?"

I frown, trying to remember that night. Was she doing that? It's hard to recall, especially since I had a few too many drinks and was feeling sorry for myself because my friends were all finding their soulmates and I hadn't. But now I have. Maybe it's all bullshit, but I truly believe Katie is the one God meant for me to have.

Not wanting to talk about Sharleen and her tits, I shake my head. "Do you want to share with the class why you've been taking so many trips to Ireland lately? Should I be worried?"

Ronan's gaze darkens as he lifts his glass to his lips. "Paige and Tessa are graduating soon. They'll be coming back to the States."

What has that got to do with him traveling to Ireland? I knew they were graduating, but I don't know why he seems upset about it. At least with Paige being home, we can all keep a close eye on her.

"And you're feeling some kind of way about it because…?" I ask.

"Because we still don't know who kidnapped Tessa all those years ago. The bastard is still out on the streets. She's been tucked away at school, but whoever took her knows she was rescued, and they know where she lives. She's not safe here."

Ah. So this is really about Tessa more than it is about Paige.

"Tessa's parents have the means to provide security for her when she returns home. They aren't going to let anything happen to her."

He flexes his hand. "I can't believe that asshole is still alive. I should have followed the trail before it disappeared."

"No, you shouldn't have. You did the right thing. You took care of Tessa and brought her home. She needed you."

It was a dark time when Tessa returned. Declan

had Paige under complete lockdown, and she was a mess over her best friend missing. Then, when Ronan brought her back and we saw how badly she'd been abused, we went hunting for the bastard who kidnapped her. The trail had gone cold, though. We still haven't figured out who it was.

"Is Tessa planning to move back in with her parents? Or do she and Paige want to get a place of their own?"

Ronan laughs. "You think Declan is going to allow Paige to live anywhere but on the estate?"

That's true. I don't blame him. It's safest for her here.

"Why not have a house built for the girls and let Tessa live there with Paige?"

His gaze snaps to mine before he rises and sets his glass down so hard that the liquid sloshes over the side. "That's fucking brilliant." Then he strides out of the room.

Shaking my head, I pull out my phone and bring up the coffee shop cameras to make sure Katie has left. Once I confirm she has, I check the location of the tracker I dropped in her purse today. When I get her moved in, I'll have trackers installed in all her shoes and clothes. My girl won't move an inch without me knowing where she is.

Cali comes bouncing into the room with Scarlet on

her tail. By the look on their faces, I know they're up to something.

"Grady," Cali says as she practically jumps onto the couch beside me. "Daddy said Katie's coming to the estate tonight, so we were wondering if she could come over and do diamond art with us while we watch a movie."

I narrow my gaze at them. "What makes you think I want to share Katie with you two? Maybe I want her all to myself."

Scarlet snorts. "Of course you do. You're all a bunch of greedy men. But we want to get to know her. Soon, she'll be living on the estate, so we need to make sure she knows we're her friends."

Okay, maybe they aren't total brats. They have good hearts, and knowing that Katie has spent so much of her life taking care of her parents, I suspect she hasn't had the chance to make a lot of friends. She needs them. While I might regret it, Cali and Scarlet are right.

"Fine. If she's feeling up to it, I'll bring her over for dinner, and then you guys can hang out afterward. She works a lot, though, and if she seems tired, I'm going to put her to bed early. Got it?"

"Yes," they say in unison.

"Good. Now, both of you need to clean up the silly string mess you made in the foyer before Grace sees it."

Cali glares at me. "Why do you assume it was us? You act like all we do is get into trouble."

The corners of my lips twitch. I reach out and delicately pull a slimy piece of silly string from her hair and hold it up in front of her. Cali's mouth falls open while Scarlet covers hers to keep her giggles quiet.

"Fiiiiine," Cali whines. "We're going. Nobody likes a know-it-all, though."

I chuckle and roll my eyes, then follow the girls through the house. As I pass them, I press a kiss to the top of each of their heads.

"I love you both."

"We love you too!" they sing happily as they start scooping up colorful pieces of whatever the fuck that stuff is.

MY GIRL DOESN'T LISTEN VERY WELL.

I watch as she pulls her purse and a tiny backpack from her car. I guess she'll be getting a lesson in obeying her Daddy tonight before bed because there definitely isn't more than one change of clothes in there. Good thing I already went shopping and had a bunch of new stuff delivered this afternoon.

As soon as she sees me, her face splits into a grin. "Hi."

Sliding my hands into my pockets, I lean against the doorframe. "Hi, baby girl."

I wonder if Tom told her about me cornering him. I suspect she would have called me and told me off if he had. She's protective of the older man.

"Where are the rest of your bags?" I ask with a raised brow.

She slows her steps, and her eyes go round. "This is all I brought."

"Really? Didn't I tell you to pack several outfits?"

My cock twitches as she pulls her plump bottom lip between her teeth. "I figured if I needed more clothes, I could run home and grab them whenever. It's not that far."

I take a step off the porch. She swallows and watches me like a hawk as I move toward her.

"When I tell you to do something, I expect you to obey. There's no reason for you to go home and get clothes when you can stay here and have all your things here."

She tips her head back to look up at me. I lower my face to hers and give her a gentle kiss, then cup her chin firmly in my hand. "Did you disobey me on purpose, princess? Are you trying to test the boundaries with me?"

"No," she whispers, her blue eyes sparkling like

rare sapphires under the outdoor light. "But I don't live here."

I smile down at her, rubbing my thumb over her jaw. "That's where you're wrong, Katie-baby. You can keep your apartment for as long as you need to feel comfortable in our relationship, but starting today, this is your home."

Part of me wants her to argue with me so I can list all the reasons she should live with me and why we're perfect for each other, but once again, she makes me fall even deeper in love with her.

"What if I want to paint it pink?" she asks, her expression serious.

"Let's go to the paint store. What shade of pink do you want?"

Her mouth falls open. "I was kidding!"

"I wasn't. I want you to make this your home. Make it comfortable. Make it what you've always imagined your house would look like. I don't give a fuck about any of that shit. The only thing I care about is having you in my bed every night so I can wake up to you every morning."

"Oh." She blinks several times, and I worry I might be putting too much on her too soon.

"Come on, baby girl. Let's go inside. I'll give you a tour, then we can decide what we're going to do tonight."

16

KATIE

By the time I'd gotten back to my apartment, I'd told myself that Grady had only said all of those amazing things because he was in the moment. I should have known better. Grady doesn't say anything he doesn't mean. Moving in, though? This soon? I want to talk to Chloe about it and ask her what she thinks. Will I regret it?

He did say I could keep my apartment for as long as I wanted. That's considerate of him. I've never lived with a man other than my dad before. What if I'm bad at it?

"Baby."

The single, gentle word relaxes me, almost like a soothing touch to my soul. "Yeah?"

Wrapping his hand around the back of my neck, he

gives me a light squeeze. "It's all going to be okay. Let's go slow. We're going to be great together."

"Okay."

"Good girl." He closes the front door behind us, and the light click of the lock settles me.

I'm not sure what I was expecting Grady's home to look like. I guess I didn't think about it too much, but as I look around at the soft gray walls and muted décor, it feels perfect for him. He leads me down a hall, and we pass a set of stairs.

"Upstairs, there's an entertainment room, several guest rooms, a couple of linen closets and bathrooms, and an empty room that you can turn into whatever you want. Our bedroom is down here, along with the library and a couple of offices. And, of course, the kitchen and living room."

I nod and glance at the pictures hanging on the walls. All of them look to be of Ireland. When I come to a photo of four people, I stop. A man and a woman have their arms around two young boys, smiling like they're all so happy just to be together. It's beautiful and heartbreaking at the same time.

"That's my parents and my brother. It was taken only a few days before they were killed." His voice comes from right behind me. I lean into him, finding comfort in the warmth of his body.

"I'm so sorry, Daddy," I whisper as tears fill my eyes.

I'm not sure if I'll ever be able to think about what Grady went through without feeling the overwhelming urge to cry. It's amazing that he turned out to be so wonderful and kind.

He slides an arm around me and pulls me back so his chin rests on top of my head. "Thank you, baby. I've had a hole in my heart for a long time, but now I feel like you're filling it and making me whole again."

Wow. I could say the exact same thing about him. It felt like the moment I met him, my world was right again.

"Come on, I want to show you the rest of the house." He holds out his hand and leads me into a huge, open living room and kitchen. The granite countertop sparkles under the black metal chandelier that's hung over the large island. Sheesh. The kitchen is a baker's dream come true.

"Your house is gorgeous. It's so comfortable and homey. I love it." I turn in a circle, taking everything in, and when I face him again, he grins.

"It's yours too, baby girl."

My heart flutters, and a flush rises to my cheeks.

He takes my purse and small backpack, setting them on the counter. "My realtor is going to meet you at your parents' house tomorrow morning. She's already done a drive-by of the place and thinks she knows a buyer who would be interested."

Relief floods me. Oh my God. That would be a huge weight off my shoulders. But…

"Really? I haven't gotten everything done to get it ready, though."

He shakes his head. "She said the list that asshole gave you is a bunch of bullshit. She'll walk through with you tomorrow and tell you what she thinks."

My lips tremble, and my tummy twists in the best way possible. If I get one more collection call from the insurance company before I have a resolution for them, I might have a full-on breakdown.

"Thank you," I say, my voice wobbly.

I'm not sure what I did to deserve a man like Grady, but I'm not going to keep questioning it.

"You're welcome. If you'd like me to be there with you, I'm happy to go."

I quickly shake my head. "No. Thank you. I need to do this myself. It's the closure I think I need."

He keeps his gaze on me, studying me for several seconds before he nods. "Okay, baby. But I'm here if you need me. It doesn't matter what I'm doing; I'll drop everything and come."

Unable to resist, I fling my arms around his waist and let out a huge sigh. "You're the best man," I murmur into his chest.

Chuckling, he wraps me up in his embrace and squeezes. "We'll see if you're still saying that after I punish you for disobeying me."

My butt tingles, and I take a quick step back. "But I didn't do it on purpose."

He moves closer, and I take another step away.

"It doesn't matter. I gave you explicit instructions, and you didn't listen."

Well, he's got me there.

"But…" I say again, trying to think of another argument. Surely, he won't spank me twice in one day.

"But, what, baby? I'm listening. You might want to start heading to the bedroom while you try to think of another excuse."

He's enjoying this. I didn't take Grady for a sadist, but I also don't hate it. I'm a little afraid for my butt, though.

"I was overthinking things, and I didn't want to assume I was going to stay here for more than one night."

Right. That's a good excuse. He'll definitely understand that one.

"Really? Even though Daddy told you specifically you'd be staying with me for the foreseeable future? Here's the thing about our dynamic, baby. When I tell you what to do, I expect you to obey. If intrusive thoughts start to cloud your mind, all you need to do is what Daddy said. It's supposed to make it so you don't have to think so much, and you can just relax and enjoy being my good girl."

"That sounds kind of wonderful, actually." I bite my

bottom lip and take in a breath. "What if there's something you say that I really don't want to do or I don't feel comfortable with?"

He gently nudges me forward. "Then you say red, and everything stops. That's during discipline and sex, too. Now, bedroom. I have something for your naughty bottom."

I yelp when he smacks my ass and scurry forward toward a hallway that leads to a set of double doors. The room is enormous. The sitting area in the corner near a set of floor-to-ceiling windows makes me want to curl up with a book on a rainy day.

"You can look around later. Right now, go to the bed and bend over the edge."

My heart skips faster, but when I turn around, he doesn't look angry or upset. He stares down at me lovingly, a soft smile playing on his lips.

"You're going to spank my poor butt again? It still hurts from earlier."

That might be a little dramatic. It's more sensitive than anything. Although the thought of him spanking me again sends a thrill down my spine right to my core. Why was it so hot being punished by a man in a black suit with tattoos all over his body? I'll definitely be fantasizing about that for many years to come.

"I didn't say anything about spanking you. Now, do as I said, or I'll restrain you."

Oh, crap. I hurry to the edge of the bed and bend over, taking just a second to soak up the silky bedding against my face. The fabric smells like Grady, which comforts me.

"Good girl. See, that wasn't so hard, was it?" His voice is laced with amusement, and I can't help but giggle softly. He is such a big meanie. A hot one and a fun one, but still a meanie.

"Daddy," I breathe.

"Yes, baby?" he asks as he reaches around to undo my pants.

When he tugs them down—along with my panties—my butt clenches. I think I want a spanking over what he's about to do.

"I'm scared."

He pauses and leans over, his gaze meeting mine. "I'll never harm you, baby. This is a punishment, but it will be a fun one. Remember, you can say red at any time and I'll stop. Understand?"

I'm in love with him.

Wow. I think I knew I was falling hard, but I'm actually deeply in love with Grady O'Brien. Since the first day we met, all he's done is take care of me, just like he is now by reassuring me how safe I am with him.

It's far too soon to tell him because the last thing I want to do is scare him away. He's the first man I've ever felt this deeply for. I doubt men like him want women getting clingy and all that.

"Yes," I whisper. "I understand. Thank you, Daddy."

The corners of his lips tip up into a smile before he presses a kiss to my mouth. He strokes my lower back and uses his tongue to explore while I do the same. Sometimes, he can be so sensual, and other times, he's rough and wild. I love it all, and I hope it never changes.

When he pulls back, he strokes my hair away from my face. "Ready?"

Heat rises to my cheeks. "Are you going to stick something in my butt?"

My question must catch him off guard because he stares at me for a beat before he throws his head back and laughs. "Yeah, baby girl. I'm going to stick something in your butt. It's going to feel good, though. I need you to trust me."

Taking a deep breath, I nod and do my best to relax on the mattress. "I do trust you."

He presses a kiss to my forehead. "Thank you. I'll never abuse your trust. Ready?"

I shoot him an incredulous look that makes him chuckle before he moves behind me, opens a drawer to the bedside table, then pulls out a small bottle and something he hides in his palm.

Oh, God. He's going to look at my butthole. And

put something inside of it. I've never experienced anything like this before. What if I scream? Or toot? I would absolutely die of humiliation. I squeeze my eyes shut and take inventory of how my stomach feels. Are the odds in my favor or not? That would be the worst possible thing that could happen.

"Take some breaths, baby girl. I can practically feel your panic. Trust that I'll take care of you. Always."

His velvety tone helps, and I let out a deep exhale. "Thank you, Daddy."

Despite the fact that I'm nervous as hell, I'm also warm all over and hoping he can't see how turned on I am by all of this. I'm giving myself over to him and letting him do what he wants to me. I'd wondered before if I was submissive. Based on how hot all of this makes me, the answer is pretty freaking clear.

He brings his hand to my lower back and slowly strokes down my crack. He doesn't stop at my hole, and I'm a little relieved but also disappointed. Why am I excited about this? Is it good excitement or bad excitement? I can't figure that out.

Then a drop of something cold hits my ass, and I jump. He keeps a hand on my lower back, steadying me. I whimper but am quickly distracted when he moves a finger over the tight ring of my hole and strokes it. Oh my God. That feels so weird. And good. And naughty.

"Daddy," I whisper.

"You're being such a good girl, Katie. I know you're going to take your punishment so well because you're always my good girl."

My nipples bud, and my pussy clenches. I'm quickly distracted from those two things as he starts to make slow thrusts into my ass.

It burns, but there's another sensation, too, and it's surprising the heck out of me. I didn't expect to feel such pleasure from this. Maybe it's the mix of taboo and anticipation adding to it. Whatever it is, I love it.

"One day, I'm going to fuck this ass, baby."

I shudder at the thought. His cock is huge. Probably ten times the size of his index finger, and I already feel full from that.

He squirts some more lube on my ass and starts to add a second finger. I stop breathing and grip the bed, squeezing my eyes shut.

"Let your breath out. You need to relax, baby." He pauses his movements and waits until I obey. "Good girl. Another one. Keep going."

With each one I take, he presses in deeper, stretching me around him. The more I breathe, the better it feels. Soon, I'm moaning out loud.

"I love watching your ass swallow my fingers. I can hardly wait to see my cock sinking in there."

I let out a whine of protest when he pulls his hand away, leaving me feeling empty.

"My baby likes her ass being played with," he says

as he touches something smooth and cold to my hole. "Don't worry, baby. We're not done."

He presses gently, the toy stretching me wider and wider. I wiggle, then startle when he smacks my ass.

"Naughty girl. Stay still. This is a punishment."

It might be a punishment, but it's a pleasurable one so far, and I think he's enjoying the hell out of it too. Especially considering I can see his enormous cock outlined in his pants when I look back at him.

"Deep breath in and then out."

I do what he says. As I exhale, he presses on the toy until it pops into place. Suddenly, I'm full and hornier than ever.

"That looks so pretty, baby. I'm going to have to invest in a princess plug with real diamonds at the base. I'll have you wear it for me with nothing else on."

Holy espresso beans. Grady is kinky. Hell, maybe I am, too, considering I'm loving every second of this.

"Crawl up onto the bed, baby. On your hands and knees."

When I don't move, he smacks my ass again. "One. Don't make me get to three, Little one, because this can go from fun to serious in a heartbeat."

Letting out a squeak, I shuffle awkwardly onto the bed, the plug moving inside me.

"Good girl. Turn so your head is facing the headboard and your toes facing the end. Then, lower your chest to the mattress so your perfect ass is in the air."

A blush heats my skin, but I do what he says and rest my cheek on the bed so I can look at him.

"I'll be right back. I'm going to wash my hands. Stay just like that."

It feels like hours pass as I listen to the water running before he returns. I'm sure it's only a few seconds, but the time away only amplifies my excitement. Why does obeying him turn me on so much? I've never felt submissive like this, but it comes so easy with him. Maybe because I trust him so much already.

He strips out of his clothes, leaving only his underwear on, then grabs something from the nightstand that I can't see. When he steps up to the bed, his bulge is right at eye level. He pulls his cock free and slowly strokes it.

"You're going to be a good girl and suck my dick while I play with your pretty pussy, aren't you?"

I lick my lips and shift my gaze to his face. "I might not be good at it."

He raises his eyebrows. "Why wouldn't you be good at it, baby? Your mouth is perfect."

"I've just never done it before."

"You've," he says, his words slow and controlled, "never sucked a man's dick before?"

"No."

His pupils go wide, and he rolls his head back, murmuring something in Gaelic.

When he looks down at me again, he's almost

angry. But then he nudges my mouth with the tip of his cock.

"Open your lips and suck like a lollipop. Watch your teeth."

I do exactly what he says and moan as a salty bead of his arousal touches my tongue. I lick and suck, stretching my mouth open as wide as possible to let him in.

He groans and gently pets my hair, closing a fist around a chunk of it every so often. He doesn't push me, though, instead letting me take my time.

I get into a rhythm, then startle as he presses something to my clit. Vibrations pulsate through my core, and I nearly scream, but I can only gag as the tip of his cock touches the back of my throat.

Every time he puts pressure on my clit with the vibrator, I jolt, and my asshole clenches. My body tenses. I'm so incredibly close to coming, but he pulls the toy away time and time again. I moan around him, but he chuckles and thrusts his hips, gagging me on the crown of his dick.

"This is a punishment, sweetheart. Did you think I was going to let you come so easily?"

I flick my gaze to his, pleading with my eyes. He winks at me and holds a handful of my hair as he starts fucking my mouth. Tears run down my cheeks. My arousal drips down the inside of my thighs. I might actually die if he doesn't let me come.

A moment later, he puts the toy to my clit again and turns it on. He circles it and flicks through different vibration settings until my eyes nearly roll back in my head. Just as I'm on the verge of explosion, he takes it away. I whine and try to pull my mouth off his cock in protest, but he tightens his grip on my hair to keep me in place.

"I didn't say you could take your mouth off my cock, baby. We're going to have to work on you following instructions, aren't we, naughty girl?"

I nod, and he turns on the vibrator. He does this several times. Torturing me. Getting me close, then backing off. I kind of want to bite his dick, but I have a feeling I'd get a very unpleasant punishment if I did that. Besides, I'm pretty sure he's going to let me come. Eventually.

"When I tell you to do something, Katie, I expect your obedience. I don't care how big or small of a thing it might seem to be. The only time I will allow disobedience is if you use your safeword."

I bob my head the best I can. I'm not sure why I didn't do what he'd asked. Maybe subconsciously, I rebelled on purpose to see what his reaction would be.

I suck on him harder while riding the edge, trying to prepare myself for when he pulls the toy away again. He doesn't, though. Instead, he turns it up to a higher speed. Sweat coats my skin; every muscle goes tight.

"That's it, my sweet girl. You're sucking my dick so

well. Fuck, you look like an angel. I'm going to fuck your pretty mouth, and when I come, I want you to swallow it all. Put your hand on my thigh and tap if you need me to stop."

I quickly slide my arm out from under me and rest my palm on his thigh. He thrusts, holding my head in place by my hair. Every time he pulls back, I moan as the toy takes me higher and higher.

"Come, baby. Come for Daddy," he growls as he starts to thrust faster.

Almost like I need his permission, the second the words come out of his mouth, I explode. Pleasure rips through me like a tidal wave, spreading all the way to the tips of my toes. At the same time, Grady lets out a low grunt, and hot semen spurts into the back of my throat.

I drink it down, moaning as the flavor passes over my tongue. Using his free hand, he reaches over to my ass while I continue to whimper and moan through my orgasm and tugs the plug free, dropping it onto the floor beside him.

When my body stops spasming, I let out a deep sigh and relax onto the mattress, feeling like a limp pile of goo. Who knew butt play could be so hot? So dirty, yet such a turn-on.

Grady quickly tucks his softening cock into his underwear, then sits on the edge of the bed and starts rubbing my back.

"You did so well, sweetheart. Fuck, that was so beautiful. You're such a good girl. My girl. I'm so proud of you."

I blush, the corners of my lips slowly curling into a smile. "You weren't so bad yourself," I mumble.

17

GRADY

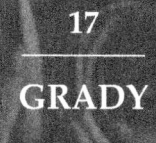

"You're late." Cali meets us at the front doors of her and Declan's house, her hands on her hips, eyes narrowed.

I raise an eyebrow. "Better watch it, brat. We can turn around and go back home."

"Noooo," Cali and Katie whine at the same time.

I'm used to that kind of thing from Cali, but hearing it from my girl has me snapping my attention down to her. She tilts her head back to look up at me, her lower lip popped out slightly.

"I want to stay," she says quietly.

The possessive side of me wants to go back home so I can have my girl all to myself, but the Daddy side of me wants to give her everything she wants. Especially since she had to give up so much of her life because she was taking care of her parents. I guess I'll have to be selfish with her another time.

"We're staying, baby. But Cali is going to quit being sassy; otherwise, I'm going to tell her Daddy that she needs a little correction from his palm."

Cali drops her hands, but she continues to glare at me. "Snitches get stitches, you know? Sometimes, they even get a pinky cut off. Do you want me to cut off your pinky?"

Smirking, I take a step toward her. "Do you know what brats get? They get their naughty bottoms spanked and plugged. Shall I go suggest that to your husband?"

Both girls gasp, but Cali quickly turns her scowl into a happier expression.

"I'm just glad you're here!" she says as she starts bouncing on her toes. "Can I take Katie to the theater room? Me and the other girls have been doing diamond art, and I have one for Katie if she wants to do some, too."

I glance down at my girl, my heart bursting as she turns her wide, hopeful eyes up to me.

"Fine, yes. Go and have fun. I'll check on you in a few."

They take off, but I quickly grab Katie by the wrist, stopping her in her tracks. I lean in to kiss her, and she wraps her arms around my waist and hugs me as I capture her mouth.

"Be good," I whisper before I let her go.

I give her a firm swat and watch them disappear down the hall. Declan's shoes tap on the white marble floors as he enters the foyer. He lifts his chin and smiles. "Cali give you an earful for being late?"

"Yes. I don't know how that's possible, considering I never gave her a time that we would be here. I don't think you spank her enough."

Declan rolls his eyes and shrugs. "She gets spanked plenty, believe me. I took a wooden spoon to her ass just a few hours ago for drinking chocolate syrup right out of the bottle. If Grace had caught her doing that, the woman would have had a heart attack. Cali's lucky I was the one who caught her."

"She drinks out of the syrup bottle all the time," Bash says as he walks up to us.

"And you've never told me?" Declan asks as he glares at his brother.

Bash shrugs. "What kind of brother-in-law would I be if I tattled on her all the time? Besides, I've had enough stitches in my life; I don't want more for snitching."

Warmth fills me inside. I didn't think I'd ever see the day when I'd be bullshitting with my family about our girls. I also didn't think any of us would ever be this happy. I just hope Ronan finds someone. I worry about him. He's been in a dark place lately, at least it seems like it. I wouldn't know for sure because he's been closed off more than usual.

"Do you mind if we have a quick meeting before dinner?" Declan asks.

"Sure. About what?" I ask.

"I want to add Patrick to the top tier, but it needs to be a group decision since it will change the structure that's been in place all this time." Declan motions toward his office.

Killian, Kieran, and Ronan are already in his office when we walk in. Ronan is scowling, but Killian and Kieran look relaxed as they sip glasses of whiskey.

"You're late," Ronan barks at me.

I grin. "Nice to see you too, man. Got up on the right side of the bed this morning, aye?"

He flips me off.

"Dude, are you going to be in a bad mood for the rest of your life?" I ask.

Killian snorts. "He's just pissed off right now because Paige and Tessa want to go to Scotland for a couple of weeks after graduation before they come back to the States, and Declan said yes.".

"They have no business traveling to another country to do God knows what. They belong here, where they can be watched," Ronan growls.

Declan rolls his eyes. "I'm sending four security guards on the trip with them. They'll be perfectly safe."

Ronan practically snarls but doesn't say anything more.

Kieran sits forward and sets his glass on the table in front of him. "What did you want to meet about, boss?"

Declan glares at Kieran, and I chuckle. He hates it when we call him boss. We love to call him that when we want to annoy him.

"I know our syndicate has always kept the top tier to six positions, but I'd like to add one more. It needs to be a group decision, not just mine."

That gets our attention. For decades, there have only been six top-ranking spots in the US-Irish syndicate. To make a change like this is big. It could also be good for us. Good for the organization.

"Who?" Killian asks.

"Patrick," Declan answers. "He's proven himself worthy. He took a bullet to protect our women. He's a good leader. He's loyal."

I nod. "He'd be a good fit. You have my support."

Everyone else agrees without hesitation. Declan wouldn't have made the recommendation without considering it from every angle. We trust his judgment. He would never do anything to put our family at risk.

"Cali and Scarlet are going to be sad they won't be able to hang out with him so much," Killian says, chuckling.

Ronan actually cracks a smile. "Aye. But the fact that he's survived those two says a lot about him. I don't think I could do it. I'd have them both tied up with duct tape over their mouths within an hour and they'd still figure out a way to annoy me."

I hold my fist to my mouth to cover my grin. Ronan's sense of humor has been absent lately, so hearing him make a joke is refreshing. Especially since he loves Cali and Scarlet so much and would never actually do anything like that to them.

Declan grins and pulls out his phone. A second later, he looks up and smirks. "Speaking of brats. They're in the middle of a diamond art fight. Again."

Bash curses while Kieran shakes his head.

I squint, trying to make sense of what that means. Declan turns the screen toward me, and I get my answer. All five women are tossing tiny fake diamonds at each other and giggling hysterically the entire time. They're making a mess. It will take forever to clean them all up. But the smile on my girl's face, seeing her have fun, I don't give a fuck how much of a mess it makes. If it makes her this happy, I'll order loads of fake diamonds for her to throw around. First, though, I need to buy her a real diamond. A big fat one that she can't say no to.

18

KATIE

I don't think I've ever felt more relieved than I do right now. I was practically on the verge of a nervous breakdown on the drive to my parents' house, especially after I got a collection call from the insurance company again.

"This house is lovely, dear. I don't think you need to do anything to it. I'm pretty sure I have a buyer who would be interested. He owns dozens of houses and rents them to families who can't afford the high rent prices in the area."

My heart warms, and I can't help but smile. "That's awfully selfless of him. A lot of landlords around the city jack up their rent prices so they can make the most profit. How does he find the families?"

Marie, the real estate agent Grady arranged for me

to meet, has been so kind since the moment we shook hands. I can see why he recommended her.

"He works with schools and veteran offices to find them. He's been doing it, gosh," she says, tapping her chin, "probably for the past fifteen years or more. He's my favorite client." She laughs, and I don't blame her. If he's purchased that many houses from her, he probably keeps her income nicely padded.

"Well, that sounds wonderful. Are you sure about the price, though? My previous agent had told me the house wasn't worth anywhere near that amount."

She scowls. I wonder how it's possible for such a sweet woman to also have such a terrifying expression. "Yes, well, Calvin is quite the scum of the real estate industry. Several of us have been trying to get his license revoked for years, but for whatever reason, it hasn't happened."

That's strange. I should probably contact the life insurance company that recommended him to me. Although, I'm not exactly impressed with their business practices either.

"Are you sure you want to sell this place, though? It's a great house," Marie says, looking around again.

I follow her gaze and let out a sigh. "It's either sell this or Twisted Bean. Though I have good memories here, the coffee shop means more to me because it was my parents' dream."

The woman gets a misty-eyed look and steps

forward to hug me. I'm surprised by it at first, but then I hug her back. This is definitely the sort of person to do business with. She actually cares. It's touching.

"I'm so sorry you're in this position. You seem to know what's most important, though, so I understand your decision. Well, let me talk to my client and see what he thinks. He's a cash buyer, so it would be a quick sale. You'd have a check within a week."

My jaw nearly hits the floor. "A week? Oh my gosh. That would be amazing. The insurance company has been breathing down my neck for me to settle my parents' hospital bills."

The scowl she had earlier returns, and she shakes her head. "Well, give me a few days and you can tell them to shove that check where the sun don't shine."

I actually snort as I burst into giggles. I throw my arms around her again. "Thank you, Marie."

She gives me a squeeze, then grabs her briefcase and heads for the front door, her sky-high killer heels clicking on the wood floor the entire way. I don't know much about BDSM, but she gives off what I'd imagine would be Dominatrix vibes. It's hot.

When I'm alone again, something settles inside me. I swear I can actually feel the weight that's been holding me hostage lift and float away.

Slowly, I wander through the house, stopping in each room to give it one last look. Memories play through my mind like a movie. Christmas mornings, pancake Saturdays with my dad, birthdays, and snow days. By the time I make it back where I started, tears stream freely down my cheeks. I miss them, but they gave me a life some people could only hope to have. They gave me unconditional love. Even on the darkest of days, no matter how sick they were, they loved me. I'll miss this place, but the thought of it being a home for someone in need makes it easier to walk out of the front door for hopefully the last time.

As I head to my car, I dig through my purse for the keys. I need a smaller purse. Or a car with one of those fob thingies, so I don't always have to dig in the endless black hole I carry around with me.

"Thought I was going to have to come in to talk to you."

My head snaps up so fast it gives me the spins. An icy shiver runs down my spine. "Calvin," I say.

"Yep," he says slowly, popping the P at the end.

Is he drunk? It's not even noon yet.

I look at my car and wince. He parked directly behind me, blocking me in.

"Can I help you with something?" I ask.

He staggers forward, and I take a step back. Shoot. He is drunk. Not only is he not walking in a straight line, but he reeks like he slept in a bourbon barrel.

"Oh, you can help me, all right. You and me, we were going to be great, doll," he slurs. "I was going to sell this piece of shit house, and then I was going to celebrate by fucking you in it."

My stomach twists. I swallow several times, trying to urge the bile to go back down. I wouldn't have fucked Calvin if he were the last guy on earth.

"But noooo," he sneers. "You sent your boyfriend and his fucking gangster friends to see me. They walked in like they owned the goddamn world. And now...*now* all of my assets are frozen, and you don't think I would put two and two together? You bitch."

I take another step back and shake my head. "Calvin, I don't know what you're talking about. I didn't send anyone to see you, and I have no idea what's going on with your assets."

He lurches toward me. Like a rabid animal trying to catch prey. I swear he's even foaming at the mouth. Letting out a scream, I try to dodge him, but excruciating pain sears through my ankle as I twist it. Unable to hold my weight, I fall backward and land on my tailbone.

Owwie.

Shit. This is bad. I need my Daddy. He'd make it better. He'd protect me. Tears burn in my eyes, blurring the world around me. Calvin looms over me, his scent burning my nostrils.

He steps forward again. I scoot back, my butt getting soaked through my jeans from the wet grass. If

I keep moving, we're going to be on the porch soon, and that's the last place I want to end up.

"I'm going to show you what it's like to be with a real man. You're going to love my dick, you fucking whore."

Calvin sways. I have to get away from him. Far, far away so I can call Daddy. Pressing my palms to the ground, I push myself up and hiss when I put weight on my ankle. Can I run? I don't think so.

As I look left and then right, trying to figure out which way is the better choice, my heart surges into my throat.

A black Escalade speeds toward us, the engine roaring with power. As soon as it comes to a stop, Grady leaps from the driver's side with his gun in hand.

"You're dead," he growls as he reaches Calvin and points the barrel right at his temple.

Calvin stumbles back, his eyes bulging from their sockets. He quickly recovers, surprising with the state he's in, and glares at Grady. "Fuck you, man."

Grady shifts his gaze to me for half a second. "You okay, baby? He touch you?"

I'm trembling so hard it takes a second to find my voice. "He didn't touch me."

Another black SUV pulls up. Bash and Ronan storm toward us. Bash comes over to me and starts inspecting me for injuries. I slap at his hands, not wanting him to touch me. The only person I want right now is Grady. I need him to pick me up and hold me and tell me everything is okay.

"No," I cry, shoving Bash away. "I want Daddy."

There's so much commotion, I don't know what's going on, but the next thing I know, Grady's in front of me, swooping me up bridal style and jogging toward his SUV.

"I got you, baby girl. Shh. I'm right here. Please stop crying. You're killing me, princess." His voice is pained and sad, but I can't stop the sobs breaking free from my lungs.

"He said he was going to…" I try to catch my breath, "to rape me."

Grady's hands tighten on me, almost to the point of pain, but I don't care. I need him. I need to feel secure, and he's giving me exactly that right now.

"Fuck. I should have come with you. You're never doing anything alone again. Never. He's dead, baby. I'm going to kill him."

The panic in his voice makes me pull back to look up at him. Pain twists his face, but I don't think it's physical. He's blaming himself.

"I'm okay. He didn't do anything," I say quickly.

"It doesn't matter. He showed up here. He intended to hurt you," he growls back. "He's a dead man."

A shiver works its way down my spine. I've never heard him sound so threatening. So scary. Yet, I've never felt safer or more relieved.

19

GRADY

I could have lost her. Who knows what that asshole would have done to her if I hadn't decided to drive down the street in front of her parents' house to check on her. I'd already driven past three times, but Marie had still been there. Then, the fourth time, I was just turning the corner and saw my girl in the front yard, struggling to get away from that asshole. I'd hit the speed dial on my car's smart screen to send my location to the guys. Thank fuck Ronan and Bash were already out and somewhat nearby the same location.

If Bash hadn't pulled me away from Calvin and told me Katie needed me, I probably would have blown his brains out right in the fucking yard. I know without even needing to ask that Bash is taking Calvin to a warehouse and will hold him there until I show up to finish him.

"Call the doc and have him meet us at the estate. I want him to check her over."

Katie looks up while Ronan drives us home in my SUV. "I'm fine. I don't need a doctor."

Ronan smirks at me in the rearview mirror. I ignore him and stroke her hair. "You're getting checked over by a doctor. You don't have a choice. Your ankle is swollen, and I want to make sure you didn't break any bones when you fell."

"I think I would know if I broke a bone."

I raise an eyebrow and stare down at her, my jaw flexing. "Now isn't the time to sass me, baby. You're seeing a doctor."

She chews on her bottom lip for a second before she sighs and lays her head down again. I'm relieved she isn't continuing to fight me because it wouldn't end well for her. When it comes to her health and safety, I will always win. The fact that I already failed to keep her safe is gutting me. I'll never forgive myself for it. She'll be lucky if I even let her go to work by herself from now on. In fact, I think maybe I'll learn how to run an espresso machine so she can't burn herself anymore either.

Ronan starts making calls, but I tune him out and focus on my girl. She's shivering. I squeeze her tighter even though it's not cold in here. Fuck, I hate myself right now. I should have been with her. Why didn't I insist on going with her?

"I'm so sorry, baby," I whisper.

She tenses and tilts her back, her blue eyes sparkling. "You have no reason to be sorry. You saved me."

My heart pounds, and a lump swells in my throat. I don't know what I ever did to deserve her, but I'm never letting this angel go.

"Marry me."

Seconds pass. Panic rises from the pit of my stomach. Shit. Why did I blurt that out? She deserves a proper proposal. Not when she's injured and scared.

"Okay." Her voice is soft but steady.

Did I hear her right?

"Okay?"

She nods. "Yes. I'll marry you. Life is too short, and I'm in love with you, so yes."

Ronan grins back at us in the rearview mirror. I'm so stunned that I can't speak. So I don't. Instead, I kiss her. Hard and deep. She returns as much as I give. Neither of us care that we're not alone. We just need each other. My entire purpose in this life is now Katie.

"I love you, baby girl. So much," I say, resting my forehead on hers. "You'll never go another day without knowing how much you mean to me."

She sniffles and wraps her hands in my shirt. We sit in silence for the remainder of the drive. When Ronan pulls up in front of Declan's house, our doctor, Declan, Killian, and Kieran all rush out to help.

I scoop her up and carry her inside to the medical room we have set up. Normally, it's used for removing bullets and stitching up stab wounds. Maybe we need to have another room just for when the girls need a doctor. Something that isn't so sterile. I'm sure Declan will agree when I bring it up to him.

"Baby, this is Finn." I motion to the doctor. He smiles at Katie. If I didn't need him to check her out, I'd probably tell him to kick rocks and stop looking at my woman. I'll save my jealousy for another time.

"You twisted your ankle pretty badly, huh?" Finn asks as he squats down in front of us.

I have her on my lap in one of the chairs because I can't bear to part with her and put her on the exam table. As much as she needs me to be strong, I'm shaken to my core, and she's my comfort.

Finn gently pulls her shoes off and rolls up her leggings so he can examine her. She's already swollen, and a bruise is forming.

After a few seconds of pressing on different parts of her foot and leg, he rises and goes to the small refrigerator under a long counter. He grabs an ice pack and gently lays it over her ankle.

"You're going to be fine. Stay off it for at least twenty-four hours and then only walk if you feel comfortable. Ice packs and elevating it will help with the swelling."

20

KATIE

"Daddy, I'm fine. I'm ready to get out of bed. It's been three days."

I love him. So much. More than anything. And I'm going to keep reminding myself of that so I don't put a pillow over his face while he sleeps.

The over-the-top thing was hot a few days ago. Now, I'm not so sure. He hasn't let me walk at all. He's carried me everywhere—not that he's actually let me get out of bed much. I was lucky he left the bathroom while I used the toilet.

"I like you right where you are. I can keep an eye on you there."

Rolling my eyes, I sigh.

"Did you just roll your eyes at me, Little girl?

Because you don't have to stand for a bare-bottom spanking."

Sheesh. I didn't think Grady would be such a strict Daddy, but he continues to surprise me every day.

Thankfully, his phone rings, distracting him from his threat. When he pulls it from his pocket, he frowns. He's been doing that a lot lately.

"What's wrong?" I ask softly.

He shakes his head, his jaw flexing. "Nothing."

My chest tightens. "I thought it was against the rules to lie. Or is that only a rule for me?"

His head snaps up, his gaze meeting mine. I shrink back slightly. Shoot. I crossed a line. I'm usually his good girl. Surely, a man like him won't handle me talking back to him well.

Then he drops his shoulders and lowers himself onto the edge of the bed, facing me. "You're right. Lying is against the rules for both of us."

I don't say anything, so he continues. "I went on a date with a woman before I met you. It was horrible. I told her I wasn't interested in seeing her again, but she's continued to call and text me, even though I've told her repeatedly to stop."

Something like heartburn settles in my chest. A woman keeps calling him? My Daddy? Oh, hell no. Nope. I've given up a lot of things in my life, but I'm not giving up this man.

"Give me your phone." I hold out my hand.

Without hesitation, he unlocks it and hands it over.

"I've only messaged her to tell her to stop contacting me. You can look at our text exchanges."

God, I love this man. He's trying to reassure me. He doesn't need to, though. I trust him. What I don't trust is the bitch who isn't respecting his boundaries. And I'm going to put a stop to it right now.

I navigate to his call log and tap on the most recent. Sharleen.

"Hey, stranger. It's about time you called me," a sickeningly, sugary-sweet voice answers.

"Hello," I reply with an edge. "If you were expecting Grady, I'm afraid he's busy. I thought, since you keep calling, you must be super excited to meet me. His fiancée. I'm Katie! And you are?"

Grady rolls his lips in and brings his fist up to his mouth to keep from chuckling. He doesn't try to take the phone from me or tell me to hang up. Nope. He's going to let me handle this and stake my claim on him. I'm so turned on by it.

"Oh, um, his fiancée?" she squeaks.

I grin. "Yes. His future wife. You must be Sharleen?"

"He told you about me?" she asks, her tone full of hope.

"Yes. As a matter of fact, he did. Would you like to know what he told me?"

Grady stares at me, letting me handle the situation.

I have no doubt if he thought I was getting upset, he'd step in to protect me.

"Sure. Although, you know you can't always believe everything a man says." Sharleen cackles, clearly thinking she's hilarious.

"Maybe *you* can't believe everything a man says, but I believe everything *my* man says."

Sharleen scoffs so loud I can't help but laugh and shake my head. This woman is something else.

"Stop calling and texting Grady because if I have to talk to you again, I'm not going to be so nice next time. He's mine. Are we clear, or do I need to spell it out for you to understand?"

I'm not a mean girl. I don't like mean girls. I think the world needs more kindness in it. But when it comes to my Daddy, I think I'd surprise even myself with how nasty I might become.

"Okay. Gosh. No need to be such a bitch," she snaps.

"Actually, there is. He already asked you to leave him alone, and you didn't. So now you get to deal with me."

The line goes dead, and I roll my eyes as I hand the phone to Grady.

He takes it and moves closer. "Did you really just do that for me?"

I shrug. "You're mine… Just like I'm yours. Right?"

The way he beams at me warms me from the inside out. We belong to each other, and while he might be my Daddy and be the one in charge, he's never going to make me feel like I'm less.

"Yes, baby girl. Exactly right. And I think it's time we make it official." He reaches into the inside of his jacket and pulls out a tiny black box. Suddenly, it's hard to breathe.

"You deserve a proposal that's more romantic than this, but I'm too impatient. I promise to do a million romantic things for you later, but I need my ring on your finger and your last name to be changed to mine as soon as possible."

All I can seem to do is bob my head as he opens the box to reveal a beautifully designed antique ring with an enormous emerald in the center.

"This was my mother's. If you want something new, I'll buy you whatever you want, but I also want you to have this. My parents loved each other deeply and unconditionally, just like I do you."

A sob breaks free from my throat. I throw my arms around him and wiggle free from the blankets to crawl onto his lap, clinging to him.

"I don't want anything else. I just want you," I cry, cupping his face as our mouths come together.

Our kiss starts soft and intimate. Without breaking apart, he slides the ring on my finger. As soon as it's on, it's like a wildfire catches, and we can't get enough of each other. He doesn't care that I haven't washed my hair in three days. Or that I haven't shaved, either. He still touches me like I'm perfect and kisses me like he won't survive if he doesn't.

My nipples ache against his T-shirt I'm wearing. Ever since he brought me up to our room after the doctor checked me out, he's been dressing me in his T-shirts. I've decided to make them my pajamas going forward because even though they've gone through the wash, they still smell like him, and I never get tired of it.

He grips my hips and lifts me. I straddle his lap, then he slides his hands around to my ass, squeezing tightly. I moan and arch into him, his thick shaft pressing against my core.

"Daddy," I whisper, nipping at his lips.

"What, baby girl?"

"I need you. Please. I need you so badly right now."

The corners of his lips curl into a soft smile as he meets my gaze. "My good girl for asking for what she needs. I want you to do that every time you need something."

I nod, though I'm not sure it will be something to come as naturally as it did just now. Asking for things has never been an option for me. I had responsibilities to my parents. But now, he's giving me the freedom to want and need, and it's such a beautiful feeling. It makes me love him even more than I did five seconds ago. Our romance has been so sudden, but it's been too powerful to deny.

"How's your ankle? I don't want to hurt you."

Giggling, I shake my head. "Daddy, it's been fine for like two days. Every time you take me into the bathroom, I walk on it, and it doesn't hurt. It was only a light sprain."

He narrows his eyes, his fingers digging into my ass. "You got off the toilet and walked around when I specifically told you not to?"

Whoops. Probably shouldn't have admitted all of that to him.

"Daddy," I whine lightly. "I love that you're overprotective, but I'm not fragile."

We stare at each other for a second before he finally nods. "You might not be fragile, but you're precious to me. I want to keep you in bubble wrap so I never have to worry about you again."

I cup his face in my hands, loving the way his short beard scratches my palms. "I know you're always going to do everything you can to protect me, but I also need you to let me live, too. Trust that I'm going to follow your safety rules and that you and your family will keep me and the other girls safe. I know it's scary, especially after what you went through, but we can't live our lives in fear."

He lets out a deep exhale. "You're right, baby. Just promise me you will always follow your health and safety rules to the T. You can be naughty and break any other rules but those. Okay?"

I grin. "So, I can be naughty, huh?"

That makes him laugh. Soon, I'm laughing, too. I'm not sure how a hot, sexy moment turned into us cracking up together, but it doesn't matter because this is us, and I think it's perfect.

A WEEK LATER...

"SIGN HERE, here, and here, and then we'll be all done, and the cash will be wired to your account."

I smile at Marie, who has been the absolute sweetest through this process. I'm so glad Grady introduced me to her. Part of me wishes he were here right now instead of one of his men, but the guys had a meeting to attend, so he sent a bodyguard with me.

When I reach the last line for my signature, I sigh and scribble my name, then look at the line below it. G.O. Enterprises. Hm.

I'm interrupted by my phone ringing. The number is unknown, and usually, I wouldn't answer, but something in my gut makes me hit accept.

"Hello?"

"Hello, this is Scott from the Seattle Police Department. Is this Katie Shaw?"

Fear clenches around me like a vise.

Please don't be calling about Grady. Please let him be okay.

"Y-yes, this is Katie." The tightness already wrapping around my throat makes it hard to speak. Hard to even breathe.

"I'm calling because someone set your coffee shop on fire. The damage is minimal, thanks to a homeless man who saw it happen. He was also able to catch the arsonist and hold her until we got here. We'll need you to come down since there is a broken window, though. We don't want anyone getting inside the premises."

Relief washes through me as I sag against the desk while Marie stares at me worriedly. I wave my hand in the air, trying to reassure her that everything is fine. Because it is. Grady is safe, and that's the only thing that truly matters. Twisted Bean is rebuildable.

I quickly tell the officer I'm on my way, then hang up so I can call my Daddy. I hate interrupting his meeting, but he told me that if I ever needed him for any reason at any time to call him no matter where he is or what he's doing.

And right now, I need my Daddy.

Grady is already at the shop when I arrive. He called my bodyguard and gave him strict instructions not to speed with me in the car. It seems Grady's word is law with that guy because he completely ignored me when I told him to go faster.

As soon as the SUV comes to a stop, Grady is at my door, helping me out. "The shop doesn't look to be in too bad of a shape. I already have a company coming to fix everything."

I try to look past him, but he blocks me and cups my chin. "Baby, breathe."

Nodding, I do what he says and look around as several firefighters survey the building. When my gaze lands on an ambulance, I gasp and take off running.

"Tom," I cry out as I approach.

An EMT is tending to his arm. When I take a look at it, my stomach coils, and I bring my hands up to my mouth to keep from vomiting.

"You're burned. Oh, God. What happened?" Tears run down my cheeks as I look him up and down for more injuries.

"He tried to throw a blanket over the flames to put the fire out and got burned. He'll be okay, if he lets me actually help him," the older EMT says. She's pretty and clearly exasperated by Tom, but underneath her irritation, I think there's something else there. She likes him.

"Tom! You could have been seriously hurt." I step closer and reach for him, but he brushes me off.

"You women need to quit fussing. I've experienced worse during my time overseas. Give me a wrap for my arm and I'll be on my way." His words are harsh, but there's no force behind them.

"Please let her check you out and take care of you, Tom. For me?" It's kind of low of me to guilt trip him, but he'll give in to being treated, and that's all that matters.

Grady walks up behind me and wraps his arms around my waist, pulling me against his front. I clutch him like an anchor.

"Who would have done something like this?" I ask. I just don't understand. Arson? It's a coffee shop. Who would want to burn it down? Was it teenagers pranking?

"Sharleen," Grady grits out between clenched teeth.

I whirl around and look up at him, my eyes practically popping out of my skull. "What?"

He runs his fingers through his hair. "I'm so fucking sorry, baby. This is my fault. I should have done more to get her to leave me alone."

"Where is she?" My voice is quiet and deadly. It

almost scares me, but I'm too pissed right now to feel anything other than pure rage.

"She's in the back seat of the cop car over there. She's been arrested and will be charged. My lawyers will make sure she spends time in jail."

My feet are moving before he finishes his sentence. No one is standing outside the cop car, thankfully. As soon as I reach it, I swing the back door open and reach in to grab a fistful of her hair.

"Are you fucking kidding me right now, you bitch! You try to burn down my coffee shop! You come after my man! My family is hurt because of you! I'll fucking kill you," I scream as I slam her head into the plexiglass window that divides the front and back of the car.

I'm yanked away by a strong set of arms, but I continue cursing her out, and goddamn, it feels good. One of the cops slams the door shut, but it doesn't stop me from giving Sharleen a piece of my mind.

"Easy, baby. Easy," Grady croons, his voice amused. "Fuck, you're hot when you're mad. I have half a mind to strip your pants down and bend you over the front of that cop car so I can fuck you in front of that bitch."

My pussy clenches, and my heart pounds harder. What the hell is wrong with me? That is not a hot fantasy. Well, it shouldn't be anyway.

Grady finally sets me on my feet, and I take a second to get my vagina calmed down.

"I can't believe she set my shop on fire. How did she know where I worked? Has she been stalking you? Oh my God, she probably has. I'm going to kill her."

"You talk about stalking like it's a bad thing, baby," Grady says, winking at me.

"I'm still going to kill her. Is her nose bleeding? I hope it's broken."

Grady stares at me for a second, then nods toward the officer nearby. "You didn't see or hear anything that just happened."

The officer immediately dips his chin, the corners of his mouth twitching. "Yes, sir. Not a thing. The way I see it, she had a tantrum inside the car and hit her face."

I snort. Even the cops obey Grady. Why is that so hot? And how can I possibly be thinking about wanting to fuck my man right now when my shop could've burned down, Tom got injured, and Grady has some woman stalking him? I've lost my mind. That's all there is to it. There's no other explanation.

Grady nudges me back toward where Tom is still arguing with the EMT. I turn and flip off Sharleen as we go. Grady chuckles and shakes his head, smiling down at me with nothing but love in his gaze.

"He's not going to go to the hospital to get treated. He's so stubborn." I drop my shoulders, the reality of what could have happened crashing through me like a tidal wave. Tom could have died. And I meant it when I told Sharleen that he's family.

"Stay here, baby. I'll be right back." Grady leads me to my bodyguard and leaves me with him, then goes over to where Tom is sitting on a stretcher.

I watch the two men talk, and though my heart swells for both of them, I wonder which one is threatening death on the other. Grady is a scary man, but I think Tom could be right up there with him, even at his age.

A moment later, Grady strolls back to me, his features calm and relaxed. Behind him, the EMTs load the stretcher into the ambulance with Tom still on it. Holy shit. Is he actually going to let them take him to the hospital?

"What just happened?" I ask when he approaches.

"They're taking him in to be treated. We'll meet him there. Aidan will stay here while the contractors start work and give me an update on when they'll be done so the shop can open back up."

I stare up at Grady, my mouth hanging open slightly. "You've handled everything," I say quietly. "I don't know what to do with myself."

He cups my face and kisses me. "You just relax and let Daddy take care of you. Be my good girl like you always are."

Nodding, I slide my arms around his waist and

squeeze him tightly. Our lives aren't perfect, but it's still pretty damn good, and I wouldn't trade it for anything.

21

GRADY

My girl is exhausted. She needs to be tucked into bed with her stuffed bunny to sleep for a good ten hours or so. I hate to tear her away from Tom's side, though. Ever since we arrived at the hospital, she's been sitting with him, holding his hand. It's clear the man loves her, and she feels the same. She may not have her parents around anymore, but she does have him, and I plan to make sure he's alive and well for as long as possible to be part of her life.

"Baby girl," I say softly.

She turns to look up at me, her eyes drooping. Yeah, she's tired. It's been a long day. I still can't believe Sharleen set the shop on fire. Jesus. Thank God Tom was nearby. Who knows what kind of damage would have been done if he hadn't been.

"It's getting late. We should go home so you can sleep and Tom can rest."

Tom nods and pats her hand. "He's right, Katie-girl. You need to go home and go to bed. I'll be fine here."

Katie sighs and rises from her chair, then leans over to hug the older man. "I'll come see you in the morning."

As we leave, I offer him a wave, though my attention is mainly on my girl.

Before we pull up to the estate, she's already asleep. She barely stirs when I lift her out of the car and carry her to our bedroom. It's not until I lower her to the bed that her eyes flutter open.

"I fell asleep," she mumbles.

I chuckle and kneel to pull off her shoes. "You did. You were snoring like a bear."

Her face scrunches up into a scowl as she narrows her eyes. "Nuh-uh. I don't snore."

Fuck, she's so cute. So innocent and sweet. She's also strong and fiery. I was shocked when she went after Sharleen today, but I was also painfully turned on. My girl didn't hold back, and it was hot.

"I never got to ask you how your meeting with Marie went today?"

I pull her leggings off, followed by her top and bra, loving that she doesn't try to cover her lush body from me. I'm going to spend the rest of my life worshipping her beautiful softness. Hopefully, one day, I'll watch her tummy swell with our child, and I'll love every bit of her then, too. My cock twitches at the thought.

Ignoring my dick, I go to the dresser to find one of my T-shirts for her to sleep in.

"It went so well. The money will be wired into my account by tomorrow. I can't believe it's finally sold, and I can pay off the insurance company. It's a huge relief, honestly."

When I pull the bedding back, she crawls underneath and takes Pancake from me when I offer her the bunny. She looks at the soft toy and then moves her gaze to me.

"Daddy?"

"Yeah, baby girl?"

"Do you think we could start doing Pancake Saturday together? I think I want it to become our tradition."

My heart soars to the heavens to thank her parents for giving me such a wonderful gift. I hate that they're not here anymore, but I hope they know I'm going to take the best care of her and give her the best life.

"I would love that, baby," I say tightly, barely able to speak past the lump in my throat.

She smiles softly and closes her eyes. "Me too, Daddy."

KATIE IS SLEEPING when I slip out of bed. She still hasn't moved when I emerge from the bathroom after my shower. I quietly scribble her a note, letting her know I'll be back with breakfast. It's not a lie. I just have another stop to make first.

It's a few minutes after seven when I walk into Tom's hospital room. He's already wide awake with a cup of steaming coffee, though I imagine it tastes like shit compared to the stuff he gets from Twisted Bean.

"Good morning," I say.

He studies me for a second, then grunts. "Katie still sleeping?"

I nod. "Yes. I came to talk to you privately."

"You gonna tell me to stay away from her?" he asks. "Because I won't. She's like a daughter to me."

Smiling, I lean back in my chair. The more I get to know this guy, the more I like him. Anyone who loves my girl and wants what's best for her is okay in my book.

"No. Actually, I came because I want to offer you a job and a place to live."

That seems to surprise him because he sets his coffee down and gives me his full attention. "A job? I'm an old man."

"An old man who needs to have a purpose in life. Like watching out for my girl. We have a handful of girls in our family that we keep surrounded with constant protection. I'd like to add you to the team of men."

He scoffs at that. "I saw the guy you had protecting her yesterday. I'm not in that kind of shape anymore."

I shrug. "It's not always the shape that matters. It's the heart. I know you'd die trying to protect Katie. Besides, I've researched your military career. You have skills that never leave a man, no matter how old they are. We have some of the best men in our organization, but they're young, and you can teach them things only experience provides."

Tom is a man of honor. He served his country, and he served it well. I don't give a shit if he's Irish or not, he's qualified for the position I'm offering, and Declan backed up the idea immediately. Loyalty is the most important thing in this life, and Tom has been nothing but that to Katie and her family.

He strokes his ragged beard a few times, the wrinkles at the corners of his eyes moving as he shifts his gaze around the room.

"This organization you work for. It's mafia? I'm Italian, and I'm pretty sure by the lull of your accent, you're Irish," he says carefully.

Yeah, that's just one of the reasons he's qualified.

He might be old and weathered, but his instincts are still there.

"Aye. We're Irish, but the Italians are our allies, and there is a peace pact in place among all the US syndicates. Makes things kind of boring sometimes, but we make more money that way."

Tom chuckles. "I don't know how much use I'd be, but I'll do it if it means helping to keep Katie safe. She's a good girl."

I let out a deep exhale. "She's the best girl."

"You're a good man, too, Grady."

Raising my chin to look at him, I shrug. "I wouldn't say that, but she makes me better."

"You're a good man. I knew it the first time I saw you with her. She needs someone like you in her life."

He's not her father. His approval shouldn't matter, but it does. Her father respected Tom and asked him to look out for her, so in a way, it feels like I'm getting her father's blessing.

"Thank you, Tom."

We sit in silence for several seconds.

"I came here for another reason," I finally say. "I've recently purchased a house as an investment, and I'd like you to live in it. It will be part of your compensation for working for us."

"I do just fine now," he replies.

I was worried this part would be more of a fight. At least by offering a job, he's giving me something in return for money. But offering him a house probably feels like a handout to him.

"I know you do. But Katie worries about you, and she'd feel better knowing you're in a safe, warm home. This is something I've done for dozens of low-income families and veterans. I buy homes and rent them to people who deserve them. You deserve this house. I also think it would mean a lot to Katie if you lived in this house."

"Why's that?" he asks, lifting a brow.

"Because it's the home she grew up in."

The corners of his lips slowly widen into a smile. "You bought her parents' house. She know about this yet?"

"No. I plan to tell her today. After I get you to agree to live there. She can't get mad at me for buying it if it gives you a roof over your head, right?"

He's quiet for a beat before he slaps his thigh with his good arm and laughs. It's deep and gravelly, but it uncoils the anxiety in my stomach.

"You're good," he says.

I grin at him. "I know how to get what I want."

His response is to laugh harder.

By the time I get home with breakfast, it's later than I'd planned. Tom and I talked for a while longer, and I gave him more details about the job. The doctor came in and said he'd be discharged this afternoon. Perfect timing since I have furniture being delivered to the house this morning for him.

Katie's sitting cross-legged on the floor in the living room, leaning against the couch with some papers in front of her and a cup of coffee in hand. Her hair is messy, and she's still in my T-shirt. She's the most beautiful sight I've ever seen.

As soon as she sees me, her eyes light up, and I feel like a fucking king. I hope she always looks at me like that. I hope I can be the man who deserves to have her look at me like that. I wasn't lying when I said she makes me a better man.

"Hi, baby girl. Sorry, I took a bit longer than expected."

I sit on the sofa next to her and lean down for a kiss. This is what life is all about. Moments like this. It's not about money or status or any of those materialistic things. It's this, right here.

"I missed you," she murmurs against my mouth.

"I missed you too. I think from now on, neither of us should go anywhere without the other."

She giggles and rolls her eyes. "Nice try, Daddy."

"Mm, I tried." I glance at the stuff in front of her. "What's all that?"

"Oh, well, since you were gone, I decided to check my bank account, and the money for the house had already been deposited. So, I called the health insurance company to make the payment."

I scratch my chin and slowly nod, trying to be as nonchalant as possible.

"The strangest thing happened when I called, though. They told me the bill had already been paid. Apparently, there had been a large donation made by a company called G.O. Enterprises for all the outstanding bills—over three hundred thousand." She turns to face me, sitting on her knees. If I weren't sweating bullets right now, I'd be pulling out my dick for her to suck it since she's in such a perfect position.

"You know what's even stranger? The investor who bought the house was also G.O. Enterprises." She raises an eyebrow at me, and I know she's put all the pieces together.

"Baby, let me explain," I say quickly.

Holding up her hand, she silences me. My gut twists so tight I think I might throw up. I knew this could backfire terribly, but I had the best of intentions and I hope that she'll understand that eventually.

"Thank you. I don't know what I did to deserve you, Grady O'Brien, but thank you." She throws her arms around my neck and crawls into my lap. A soft sob escapes her, and it both heals and breaks my heart all at the same time.

"I've got you, baby. I'm right here." I stroke her hair and rock her, finding my own comfort in her warmth.

Life is full of sorrows, but it's also full of joy. I think we've both faced enough sadness. Now is our time for beautiful bliss.

I hold her for a long time, neither of us saying anything. We don't need to. We know what we mean to each other. We're soulmates. There's no question about it.

When I finally speak again, I tell her about Tom, and she breaks down into tears again. We spend the next few hours in the living room, holding each other, talking, and making love. It's soft and intimate and slow. It's perfect.

She's perfect. And she's mine. Forever and always.

ALSO BY KATE OLIVER

West Coast Daddies Series

Ally's Christmas Daddy

Haylee's Hero Daddy

Maddie's Daddy Crush

Safe With Daddy

Trusting Her Daddy

Ruby's Forever Daddies

Daddies of the Shadows Series

Knox

Ash

Beau

Wolf

Leo

Maddox

Colt

Hawk

Angel

Tate

Rawhide Ranch

A Little Fourth of July Fiasco

Shadowridge Guardians

(A multi-author series)

Kade

Doc

Syndicate Kings

Corrupting Cali: Declan's Story

Saving Scarlet: Killian's Story

Controlling Chloe: Bash's Story

Possessing Paisley: Kieran's Story

Keeping Katie: Grady's Story

Taking Tessa: Ronan's Story

Daddies of Pine Hollow

Jaxon

Dane

Nash

Dark Ops Daddies

Cage

KEEP UP WITH KATE!

Sign up for my newsletter get teasers, cover reveals, updates, and extra content!

The kindest thing you can do for an author is to leave a positive review!

Printed in Great Britain
by Amazon